FROST LINE

A helpless woman is attacked in her home by a ruthless gang of murderers and thieves searching for her brother's valuable gun collection. They fail in their mission, and now they're coming back to finish the job — this time determined to leave no eye witnesses alive. Sheriff Washington Shipp must use all his instincts and expertise to track them down before they can strike again. But one of the criminals, more dangerous than all the rest, is leaving a trail of bodies across Louisiana — and Wash may be next in line . . .

ARDATH MAYHAR
WITH MARY WICKIZER BURGESS

FROST LINE

Complete and Unabridged

LINFORD
Leicester

First published in Great Britain

First Linford Edition
published 2018

A catalogue record for this book is available
from the British Library.

ISBN 978–1–4448–3921–0

Published by
F. A. Thorpe (Publishing)
Anstey, Leicestershire

Set by Words & Graphics Ltd.
Anstey, Leicestershire
Printed and bound in Great Britain by
T. J. International Ltd., Padstow, Cornwall
This book is printed on acid-free paper

Dedicated to the Memory of
Ardath Mayhar (1930–2012),
a gifted storyteller who inspired
and entertained readers for
over thirty years.

The frost line — also known as frost depth or freezing depth — is most commonly the depth to which the groundwater in soil is expected to freeze. The frost depth depends on the climatic conditions of an area, the heat transfer properties of the soil and adjacent materials, and on nearby heat sources.

1

Washington Shipp's secretary, Amy Mendoza, had stacked the morning's out-of-area dispatches neatly on his desk while he finished reading through the overnight reports from his own deputies.

Wash had learned a whole new set of skills since becoming county sheriff, for which his time as chief of police of Templeton, Texas had not prepared him. In his previous position, he had not felt the need to keep up with all the crimes taking place outside his own jurisdiction. Now he shuddered and picked up a thick new pile of print-outs, which he scanned through as quickly as possible.

Some events had taken place in areas too distant to concern him overly much. But he did find one among the sheets that gave him pause. Some knowledgeable thieves in the Arkansas-Texas-Louisiana region were stealing antique firearms, very selectively. This was the fourth incident of this kind that had crossed his desk, and Wash now felt sure that this was some sort of 'steal-to-order' ring, fencing to a dealer with nationwide or international connections. While some might have scoffed at the notion that a small town like Templeton was too remote and unsophisticated to offer much in the way of temptation for the attentions of such a group, Washington Shipp knew better.

The Frost family had been the patricians of the area ever since Wash was a small black boy growing up in the river bottoms beyond the imposing Frost mansion on the outskirts of town. Wash's grandfather had been employed by the founder of the family fortune. Livingston Frost, the grandson and heir of old Mr. Frost, still lived on the same property. He was presently one of the foremost dealers in antique firearms in the entire region. His stock, which Wash had examined back when he was police chief, was nothing less than amazing, and Stony Frost had added to his grandfather's collection by trading, buying, and selling, until it was almost unequaled — at least in this area of the country.

If the gang of thieves was as well-informed as they seemed to be, from the long list of victims and stolen items attributed to them, it was more than certain that one day they would target the guns of Livingston Frost.

Wash reached for the phone and punched in a familiar number. It rang several times before a hesitant voice said, 'Hello?'

'Miss Frost, is your brother at home? This is Sheriff Shipp, and I really do need to speak to him, if at all possible.'

The timid voice grew a bit stronger. 'Oh, Wash! I'm glad it's you. I was afraid it might be . . . some stranger. No, Stony's away at a gun show. He said he wouldn't be home until the end of the week when he called last night.'

Wash sighed. He certainly wasn't going to alarm poor Lily with this rather nebulous concern he felt. She had problems enough of her own.

No. The best he could do was to ask her to have Stony call him as soon as he returned home. A hunch wasn't enough to justify bothering Frost at his hotel or the gun show.

Wash sat for a moment after he hung up, wondering again about the woman who waited there alone in the old family home. Always shy and insecure as a child, the adult Lily was now a recluse. Yet she, of all people, had engaged in a wild and adventurous escapade during her youth that few in the area still recalled.

She had left her home in Templeton and was gone for nearly two years. No one knew where. When she returned, seeking asylum, Lily Frost was radically changed — damaged both mentally and physically — and, seemingly, beyond repair. Although he had not asked any questions at the time, Wash still wondered about what had transpired to cause such a difference in her.

He and Stony had been friendly as lads, mainly because of their grandfathers' association — but, although there was mutual respect, the two adult men were not as close as all that. Yet Washington Shipp felt a responsibility to the Frost family, just as he did to all those under his jurisdictive care. Other sheriffs, he knew, were corrupt, or unwise or simply uncaring; but he had determined, when he ran for office, to be the caretaker of his county.

Now, thinking about the gang of thieves, he felt a small shiver of apprehension. He shook it away impatiently. He could not allow his hunches to control his work.

Just then the phone rang, and the sheriff returned to his job, moving on to the complex problems that even a relatively small county in east Texas seemed to generate constantly.

★ ★ ★

Something was wrong. Livingston Frost sensed it as soon as he pulled in the drive.

It was raining. But that wasn't unusual in east Texas in the winter. Stony hated dampness and chill. His warped body ached worse in such weather. That, he thought, was making him feel so apprehensive and ill at ease as he drove into his garage.

The weather set his bones to twinging, sending stabs of agony through his small frame. The polio that had withered his left leg and twisted his back out of shape when he was nine years old also had left a legacy of pain that had been his constant companion for most of his forty-odd years.

He leaned heavily on his cane as he hurried from the garage toward the big dark house, whose dour and disapproving face reminded him of his Scottish grandfather who had built it. In the rain it all but scowled at anyone bold enough to venture onto its curving porch. But now he had no time for such whimsy, even though he often leavened his limited and joyless life with wry humor.

Lily should have the coffeepot on and a supper of hot soup, salad and homemade bread waiting. He had been gone for a week this time, attending a particularly promising showing of antique firearms, which had led to a visit to the home of an important customer — and thus had delayed his return.

His sister always missed him dreadfully

on these occasions. He was to her what she was to him, the sole companion of a lonely life. Their only living relative was miles away, very elderly, and unlikely to survive for long. As a result, they were accustomed to relying on each other for everything.

Stony never allowed himself to wonder what would happen to Lily if he should die first.

His key turned in the stiff lock, and the door creaked open, the hall breathing into his face its usual aroma of furniture polish and mildew. But there was something else lurking there — something subtly wrong with the feel of the house. His illness had left Frost painfully aware of atmosphere, and tonight his normally welcoming home was filled with something forbidding.

'Lily! Are you here?' he called out.

The place was entirely too still. She should have been in the hall as soon as his feet thumped unevenly across the porch, her tall gawky shape hurrying to greet him, her long braid flapping behind her. She endured his business trips with impatience tinged with misery.

But there was no answer from the depths of the house. The twilight outside did nothing to lessen the darkness within; and he flicked the switch for the lamps.

Nothing happened. Had the storm caused a power outage? He had noticed that the street lamps were burning in the early darkness outside. Whatever the problem was, it had to be the house's own system.

Grumbling a bit, he fumbled blindly in the drawer of the breakfront beside the parlor door and found a candle. Matches waited beside it, and he struck a light and looked about.

It seemed the storm must have swept through the interior of the house. Furniture was overturned or pushed out of place, though the mahogany Victorian pieces were too heavy to damage much. A ruby glass vase that had been his grandmother's lay shattered on the Persian carpet, blood-colored shards picking up the faint glimmers from his candle.

Frost's heart thumped uncomfortably

in his throat. His sister was extremely dear to him. Even with mental problems left over from her brief flirtation with drugs, she kept his house clean and comfortable. Her infrequent lapses into delusion were a small price to pay for her company. While he had never thought to wonder if he loved her, he knew that he *needed* her, even as she did him, to help give him some semblance of a normal life.

'Lily?' he croaked again, holding his stick now as a weapon instead of a prop.

He moved into the hall leading to the dining room and the kitchen. There was no sound from upstairs or down. Listening intently, he went along halt-ingly, trying to see into the various rooms along the crowded corridor. The candle's frail flame did little to help his search.

His stomach had curled into a tight knot, and the hand holding the candle was shaking. He had always lacked physical strength. Now he wondered if he might be a coward as well.

He dreaded entering the kitchen at the end of the corridor — and it took all his willpower to push open the swinging door.

For a brief moment, as he looked around, he believed the room was empty. If the storm had struck here, there was little that had been disrupted. But as he stared about, he spotted a fine drift of flour over part of the floor. The trail led into a shadow beyond the marble-topped work table that Lily used for making pastry and kneading bread. She lay there, a cracked bowl by her hand and the flour sifter on its side beyond her. There was blood on her forehead.

He went down onto one knee, awkward and unsure about his ability to cope with this calamity. 'Lily, oh, Lily,' he mourned, lifting her head into a more comfortable position and trying to wipe away the drying blood with his immaculate handkerchief.

She sighed and groaned, and something inside him rejoiced. She was alive! He had not been left entirely alone in the dark confines of their old home, to be comforted only by the chilly presence of his antique weapons.

And that thought brought him up short. The house did not promise wealth by its outward appearance. It looked to be, instead, what it was in actuality — a place filled with the preserved aura of Victorianism, and preserving long family traditions and possessions. Only his guns were of great value — and they were extremely valuable — although most of those in the house were renovated ones that he used for display. His most valuable stock was kept in the vault at the Templeton Bank, not here in the house.

This break-in tonight might have been the work of mere vandals. But he wondered why they would pick such a secluded neighborhood and such an unpromising old house for their shenanigans. And seldom, he was convinced, did such rascals choose to violate a home where someone might be present. On the other hand, professional thieves after his rather famous firearms collection might try to make this look like a random act of violence. That theory *did* make a certain amount of sense.

Lily groaned again. 'Martin?' she

murmured, her voice thick and unfamiliar. 'Don't hit me again, Martin!'

Frost gritted his teeth. That name had not passed her lips in twenty-some years, not since the day she had reappeared on the steps of this very house, all her possessions in a knapsack on her back. It had been instinct — the innate ability to find home again — that had brought her through the fog of drugs, out of her unstable hippie-style existence and back into the family home and his life. Then, too, she had been bruised and bloody.

If Stony had been able to find Martin Fewell at that moment in time, he would have shot him, being quite incapable of doing anything more actively physical like beating the brute to a pulp.

Lily opened her eyes, staring up from the hazed depths of her confusion. 'Stony? Is it you? They came to the door. They kicked it in. Stony, *they took your guns*!'

He helped her to sit up, fury building inside him until he was afraid his fragile body couldn't contain it. 'Who were they?' he asked. 'Did you recognize any of

14

them?' He wondered about Martin Fewell. Would he have dared show up at this house?

Lily might not be able to come up with a clear and usable description. She was definitely sharper, now that her past life had receded — but she still had periods of incoherence and lack of memory, especially following an emotional upset like this.

She sat for a moment, looking at him and putting her thoughts together, then pulled herself up to a standing position with some difficulty. Lily was taller than he, a bit heavier, and certainly not crippled. Now she helped him up off the floor, rather than the reverse. But she did it absently, her gaze fixed on some point out of the normal range.

Frost tugged at her elbow and got her into the ancient rocking chair that their mother had insisted on keeping in her kitchen, long past the days when she rocked her infants there..

'You sit here and rest. I'll make some coffee — or maybe tea would be better for you. Who was it, Lily?' he urged. 'Can

15

you identify them?' He took the kettle from beneath the sink.

'They got your guns, Stony,' she repeated. 'They got the ones on the wall in the den — and the ones in the glass case in the living room. I couldn't get up, but I *saw* them come back with them. Will this ruin us, Stony?' she asked anxiously.

Her eyes were foggy, but he thought she seemed to be gaining back some control of her faculties. He shook his head emphatically. 'No. I keep the most valuable guns in the vault at the bank,' he reminded her. 'We'll be just fine.'

She nodded slowly, but he thought she wasn't really listening to what he said.

'The big one was mean,' she murmured. 'He looked just like Martin, with a black beard like his. I bit him on the arm, the bastard!' she added a little louder.

Stony looked down at her in surprise. In all the time Lily had lived with the cruel Martin Fewell, she had never once stood up to the man, or so she'd told him. Had some unknown quantity in the quiet life they led together finally given her the backbone to defend herself — to fight back?

'How many were there?' he asked, afraid he might distract her from her unstable concentration.

'There were four of them.' She sounded more confident now. 'Two were little blond fellows, just alike. They could have been twins, maybe, although one of them had a big scar on his hand. I got a good look at it when he hit me. The fourth one, the quiet one, didn't come close enough for me to see him clearly. He was just a man in a raincoat and a wide hat shading his face. I got the impression, somehow, that he didn't want to be involved with the violence.' She closed her eyes and sighed deeply as the cut over her eye began to ooze blood again.

Stony filled the teakettle and got it going on the stove. Then he wet his handkerchief. As he dabbed carefully at the cut on his sister's face, he thought furiously. She was lucid! That was wonderful. She could describe these villains — and she might even be able to testify, if the police ever caught them. Lily was definitely getting better.

She took the wet cloth from him and held it to her head as he dialed the number for the sheriff's department. But the phone was dead — they must have cut the wires before breaking into the house, probably when they pulled the circuit breaker.

'You sit still here,' he told his sister. 'I'm going to drive up to the corner and call Wash Shipp.'

She stared at him as if trying to recall something. Then she brightened. 'That reminds me: Wash called for you the other day. He said for you to get in touch with him as soon as possible . . . but he didn't say why . . . ' Her voice trailed off as he left her to go make the call.

Stony made his way through the rain and darkness, amidst dazzling droplets studded here and there by the street lamps, to reach the car. As furious and worried as he was right now, he wondered if this shock and her renewed ability to resist might be the very thing Lily had

18

needed to bring her out of her twenty-year-long daze.

And yet he had a very bad feeling about the entire matter. These interlopers were dangerous men, he felt. Much too dangerous to meddle with on his own. He backed out into the empty street and headed toward the convenience store, chewing at his lower lip and deep in thought.

He had marked those relatively value-less rebuilt guns he displayed in the house, etching his Social Security number in hidden places. He could identify every single one of them — or any part of them — from barrel to grip strap. If, by some fluke, the police caught the scoundrels with their loot, he could nail them. And if Lily could stand up to a trial, he was sure she could identify at least three of them. He intended to hang the bastards out to dry, no matter what it took to accomplish the task.

The phone rang, and he steadied his voice, which tended to be shaky.

'Sheriff's office,' a woman answered.

'Amy?' he asked.

'No, it's Lucy,' the dispatcher replied.

'It's Stony Frost,' he said. 'Tell Wash I need to report something really serious.'

2

Washington Shipp was not a patient man, and he disliked criminals with all his might. He despised sneak thieves and vandals, of course, and he dealt with any who were caught operating in his bailiwick as sternly as the law allowed. He detested burglars, and anyone who attacked one of the people in his charge turned up his emotional thermostat to the boiling point.

He had hoped, on this rainy evening, to go home and watch TV with his nine-year-old son while his wife worked on her weekly column for the *Templeton Signal*.

The call from Livingston Frost put the kibosh on that. 'Break-in at 6411 Oak Grove Lane,' the dispatcher said as she came out of her office. 'That Frost fellow who deals in antique guns. Might be a big haul there if they got any of his choice pieces. I went to his gun show last year, and there was stuff there that would make you drool.'

Nobody would have picked dumpy little Lucy Fowler as an antique weapons enthusiast, Wash reflected. 'I'd like to get rid of every last gun in the world,' he growled. 'What does he report missing?'

'He didn't say anything about missing property. He was boiling over because the men who broke into the house hurt his sister. You know, Lily, who went off to be a hippie and came back with her wits addled.'

'Badly?' The question came so fast and so sharply that Mrs. Fowler blinked.

'Hit her on the head, he told me. I've sent Sterling and Lambert to check things out. That okay? They were patrolling only about a half a mile away.'

She was watching him, reading him, he knew. She'd known him since he was a teenager doing chores for the wealthy families in town, and it sometimes made him uncomfortable to think how closely she could predict what he'd do.

'Lucy, you know I'm going out there, don't you? My granddaddy worked for

Dr. Frost, and I've always known Stony and Lily. No matter what mistakes she made when she was young and foolish, she's a friend. I want to see with my own eyes what happened.'

She grinned, the rouge on her faintly wrinkled cheeks crinkling into pink relief. 'I've already told 'em you'd be there. Jim has your car out front, waiting for you.'

He half-chuckled as he pulled on his leather jacket. It was sometimes very handy to have your needs met before you knew you needed them, but he would have liked just once to surprise that woman! He had a feeling that would never happen, though, for she could predict things she knew nothing about and could not explain at all. It was some kind of gift, he supposed.

The roads were slick with rain; and reflections of oncoming lights, brightly lit signs, and street lamps glimmered on the black mirror of the asphalt. He squinted, trying to separate the real from the illusory. But it grew much darker as he got out into the remote area where the Frosts lived.

Oak Grove Lane had been a county road ten years ago. Only fishermen going to the river with their boats and gear had used it, or farmers bringing in produce from their low-lying farms. Woods still grew along most of its length, broken here and there by old homes like the Frost house or by a few new brick mansions, each surrounded by its own acreage of trees and grass. The Frosts had owned a thousand acres, once upon a time, reaching all the way down to the Nichayac River. It was only by selling off bits of land that young Livingston had managed to keep things together after his father died. The Frosts had been what the local people called land-poor — lots of land, but no money to speak of.

Strangely enough, it had been Lucy Fowler who had led young Frost into what became his business. She had known his father well; indeed, everyone in the county had known old Doc Frost, and most had come into the world under his gentle touch. She had shared the old man's interest in antique weapons, even before the collecting craze hit its peak in the 1970s. Lucy had pointed out to Stony that his father's and grandfather's gun collections might be worth a great deal of money — and that advice had set him on the road to financial independence. Now his trading, buying, and selling were a part of the intricate network of antique firearms collecting in this part of the United States, and had become, Wash knew, a highly profitable business.

And that, once he thought about it, scared the sheriff half to death. He already had the notion that there might be 'special order' thieves who knew where anything could be found, and who took orders and delivered the goods as dependably as Sears, Roebuck ever had. The difference was that their stock was stolen to order.

The road curved to miss a huge maple that leaned over the way. The Frost driveway looped to the left, just past the tree, and a dim glow shone through the dripping privet and holly hedge to guide him into the parking area before the garage.

A police car was pulled off to one side,

and Frost's own modest Toyota was halfway inside the shelter. Shipp slammed his door and strode across the wet gravel and onto the haven of the porch. The lamp had been lit, and although it contained half a dozen bulbs, the total wattage was probably something like fifty, he decided.

The door opened before he could knock, and young Whit Lambert nodded as he stepped back to let him enter. 'Lucy said you'd probably be coming, Sheriff. They made a mess of the place, all right. Broke some antique glass, and scratched up the furniture a mite. We were able to find the circuit box and get the power back on, which helps. The lady isn't hurt much, but Mr. Frost's display guns were all taken.'

Wash's scowl reflected his feelings on that score. Not that he believed that the antique weapons would ever be used by the thieves — there were more efficient weapons, to be stolen far more easily. But the mere possibility gave him the shivers.

He followed Lambert down the dark hallway toward the kitchen, where the smell of percolating coffee was beginning to warm the air. Lily was sitting in a Lincoln rocker, sipping a cup of tea, and Frost was perched on a stool, his thin face paper-white, his hair curled from the damp. He stood as the sheriff entered.

'Wash! Glad you came. I've been trying to persuade Lily that what was stolen isn't my real stock, just my rebuilt models for show, so to speak. Maybe you can make her accept that. She's always listened to you.'

Shipp took the proffered kitchen chair and turned it to straddle the seat. 'I don't know about all that myself, Stony. Maybe you can tell it again, and we'll see if this time around it will make sense to all of us.'

'Oh.'

Frost seemed at a loss for words for a moment. Then he nodded, climbed back onto his stool and ran a slender hand through his thinning hair. 'All right, I'll try. Well, to begin with, I keep all my most valuable stock in a vault down at the bank. My dad did that before me, and even Granddad had begun storing his best pieces there when they built that storage facility for large valuables — although the real collecting fever hadn't yet hit — nor had the trade in stolen antiques. So what I had displayed on my walls and in my cabinets here were either replicas — which aren't worth much at all — or rebuilt weapons that had deteriorated so much I had to replace too many parts to allow them to be sold as really good antique specimens. You following all that?'

Shipp nodded. 'Sounds logical to me,' he said. 'You could show the replicas to your customers, just to give them an idea of what you had; and then, if they were interested, you'd get the real thing out of the vault and sell it to them.'

'Right, that's exactly how it worked. But still the pieces here weren't completely worthless. They were valued at about $3,000 in all, I'd guess, for my insurance policy. That isn't much per item, but it's enough to make this grand larceny, isn't it? I want to nail those bastards with everything I can. They *hit* Lily, Wash!'

Wash, despite himself, had always had a certain innate contempt for weakness, no matter what its cause. And he had always regarded Stony Frost in that regard. Now, he looked at the other man with a new respect. The fellow couldn't help being crippled. And now he was as mad as a wet wasp, ready to go to war, it seemed.

'We're going to get them,' he said. 'Don't you worry about that.' He turned to Lily. 'Can you tell me what they looked like, Lily-bird?'

She looked up for the first time, the old nickname rousing her as nothing else had done since he arrived. 'Washington? You're here? That's nice . . . ' She drifted away again.

Frost left his stool to kneel beside the rocker, his withered leg making a hard job of it. 'Lily, honey, tell Wash what they looked like, okay?'

She stared down at him, then raised her eyes to the sheriff. 'All right,' she sighed. 'One was big — really tall — and he had a dark beard. He looked quite a bit like Martin, Wash — *he looked like Martin . . . Fewell.*'

That told Wash a great deal, for he had known Martin Fewell pretty well when they both were boys. Wash had taken an instant dislike to Martin that grew worse and worse over the years, culminating in the day Martin got drunk, came to town and picked a fight with him in the drugstore. When Lily had run off with the fellow, Wash had been certain his friend was making a big mistake, and he had not been proved wrong. And he knew what Martin looked like. Yes, indeed.

'Do you think he was some relative of Martin's?' he asked Lily.

She shook her head. 'I have no idea, Wash. If he is, he's a relative I've never met.' She continued, 'Then there were two smaller men, both blond, twins I think. They had narrow little faces like foxes, and one had a scar — you tell him about it later, Stony. I'm tired.'

'Three then — that was all you saw?'

'No. There was another one, but he was all wrapped up in a raincoat, with a big wide hat over his face, and I couldn't see him real well. He didn't come close to me at all. I don't think he wanted to be seen . . . ' Suddenly she fell back in the chair, drained, and the trail of dried blood running down her cheek and beneath the bandage made her look like the survivor of some terrible disaster. Which, in a way, she was, Wash thought.

'Lily, can you tell me for certain that these were the men, if I call you to testify? If we catch them, will you be able to identify them?'

He watched her face closely as she considered. 'S-sometimes I'm scared, Wash. I'm so scared I go and hide in my room for days. But I'll try. This time I'll try.'

'I think that's enough, Miz Lily,' Wash said. He looked up at Frost, still perched like a wise old bird on his stool. 'Come in the other room and talk to me about the guns, Stony. We can let your sister rest now.'

Inside, the sheriff was boiling mad. Any bastard who thought he could sneak into Washington Shipp's county, break into houses and beat lone and defenseless women should have another think coming. Such an individual would pay a heavy price for such gall.

Wash took down every scrap of information the Frosts could provide. Then he went around the house, inside and out, making copious notes while the fingerprint man did his job. They ended up with a couple of dabs on the circuit box that were neither Lily's nor Livingston's, probably because the metal latch was old and rusty, and would be difficult for a stranger to open while wearing gloves.

By the time his investigation was completed, Washington Shipp had a good idea of what his next steps would be. Back at the office, he had Lucy send out a region-wide bulletin using all the descriptions he had. Then he sent the odd fingerprints to the FBI — along with a complete list of the identifying numbers and features of all the stolen guns.

He had a feeling the culprits were already out of the area — but he also had a gut instinct that they might well come back, sooner or later, once they discovered that the guns they had stolen were relatively worthless. Then they might well try again.

* * *

The black van sped quietly down the deserted state highway, tearing a bright trail of light through the seamless darkness of the countryside.

This route was busy enough in the daytime, but at night few vehicles used it. Occasionally, tiny hamlets provided the only swift points of light amid the long stretches of forest and pastureland that lined the way.

Myron Duson (pronounced Cajun-style, Dew-so) knew just about every inch of back road in all of east Texas and the western half of Louisiana. He always planned his jobs carefully, and he prided himself on never leaving any loose ends — which was why he was feeling so uncomfortable now.

'You sure that bitch was dead?' he asked for the third time in the past five miles. 'She kept starin' at me like she knew me somehow. Made me mighty

33

nervous, like she'd know me again if she saw me. Didn't seem to me you hit her quite hard enough, Dave.'

David Crowley didn't turn his head as he replied, 'Myron, you're gettin' old and scary. 'Course she's dead. I hit her a lick, I tell you. Besides, we're clean out of that country now, and we'll be in Shreveport before you can say scat. Our client is going to go ape over these guns we got.' The dim light from the dash showed the small man's profile and a straggle of pale hair.

Myron sighed and looked back at the road. Something had gone sour, and he wasn't able to put his finger on just what it might be. 'You got the scanner hooked up yet?' he asked over his shoulder.

Donald Crowley, Dave's twin brother, grunted behind him. 'Here, Dew. It's hooked into the power supply.' He handed the device over. 'Listen to me good, now. You're gettin' all shook over nothin'.'

There came a click, and the hum of the scanner was broken by a distant chatter of talk. A stronger signal brought a string of directions and code numbers. Then, the statement Duson was dreading: '*All Points Bulletin. Repeat All Points Bulletin. Wanted: for assault, breaking and entering, and grand theft, four men, probably traveling together, descriptions as follows: One male Caucasian, over six feet, heavy-set, dark hair and beard, black eyes, and dark complexion. Two male Caucasians, possibly twins, blond hair, narrow faces, scar on back of right hand of one shaped like a W. One male, probably Caucasian, tall, physique and coloring uncertain, wearing a trench coat and hat with wide brim.*'

'By God, I *told* you that you didn't hit her hard enough!' Duson shouted at Crowley over the rumble of the engine. 'That woman's still alive all right, and Frost got back and found her. Now we're goin' to have every cop over both states huntin' us down like animals!' He slowed to the speed limit, and the noise of the engine quieted a bit.

'If her head is that hard, you couldn't have dented it yourself,' David snapped. 'Here, turn right up at the next crossroad.

There's a dirt road I know that will take us over to Highway 21. That'll get us over the state line, and from there it's just a hop, skip, and a jump to Shreveport. We can circle off to the east and hit our man's driveway without going onto the main highway again.'

The van slowed still more, and within a half hour it was bumping along over the ruts of a muddy country lane. Sure enough, in a couple of hours it ended at the narrow pavement off 21, and they turned with great relief toward the Louisiana line.

But Myron Duson was not a happy man, even though they were closer now to their target. They hit Route 171 to Shreveport by midnight, and heard no more bulletins out on them, once they crossed over into the next state.

He relaxed a bit then. Things were going to be all right, he reasoned, and this special order would be delivered on time and in fine fashion. The broker should pay a good price for the pieces stashed in the back of the van.

He snorted and shifted his position.

What anybody would want with a bunch of ancient guns that probably would blow up in your face if you tried to fire them, he didn't know. The polished stocks, the elaborate engravings on barrels and plates, the loving care with which they had been made and used didn't impress him. A good sound Uzi, now, could make tears come to his eyes. This stuff was a bunch of crap.

They bypassed the main part of Shreveport, approaching their goal from the southeast. Bollivar's drive was hard to find in the dark — or the daylight, for that matter — but Duson hit it unerringly. The van pulled out of sight among the overhanging crepe myrtles and mimosas, and he came to a stop in a garage behind a trimmed privet hedge.

As soon as the engine died, a light came on. The outer doors closed silently, providing cover for the transaction that was about to take place. Myron opened his door and got out. His knees were stiff with the damp and from sitting for so long.

'Easy haul?' asked a disembodied voice,

and a thin figure appeared, outlined by the light from a door connecting the garage with the residence beyond.

'Not so's you'd notice,' said Myron sourly. He unlocked the rear doors of the van and pulled them open wide. 'There was a damned woman in there — nobody told me Frost lived with somebody. We walked right in and there she was in the kitchen. Couldn't see any light from the front at all. Made it a sticky proposition, I tell you.'

The other man stiffened, his pale eyes narrowing. 'And . . . ?' he asked.

'Dave hit her. Not quite hard enough. There put a bulletin out on us, back there in Texas. Probably no word out here. At least, not yet.' Myron Duson was upset, and the tone of his voice reflected his disgust.

The man known as Bollivar relaxed just a bit. 'Might as well check out the goods,' he said, moving to peer into the darkness inside the van. 'You in there. Frenchy. Hand me whatever's up on top.'

A dark-skinned hand came into view, holding an oddly shaped gun wrapped in plastic. Bollivar slipped the plastic off and eyed the piece. His eyes lit up, but Myron knew that it was with greed, not with the collector's true fanaticism.

'This looks like a Wesson sport rifle. Short barrel. It's in really fine condition — I think I can get a good price for it. If the rest come up to this one, you're going to be able to take off for a while and let things cool down.'

The other twin had crawled out the front, and now the last man came sliding out the rear of the van. 'Don' you go foolin' yourself,' he said. His yellow-brown eyes were filled with wicked amusement in the stark light of the garage.

'I been looking, back there, wit' my little flash. These is all real, yes and true. But they not what you want, Meester Bollivar. These is for show, they not for sale. Not to collector, you bet.' He chuckled, his face wrinkled with glee.

'What would you know about what collectors want?' the broker asked, his mouth tight.

'Old Maurice, he be in the business for

a long time, man. I work wid him when I be a boy. Maurice, he know a hawk from a handsaw any day of the week. He know jewel, he know gun, he know old furniture, he know everything anybody want, any time, any place. An' he teach me. You look at those gun. Every piece be mark; you look. That Fros' man, he too smart to risk his business in that old rattletrap house that anybody get in with two hairpin and a strong breath of air.'

Bollivar was frowning now, and Myron felt as if he himself might burst. The Crowleys stood off to one side, their heads cocked in opposite directions, as if they were mirror images. Their identical faces held no expression.

The broker's fingers moved surely, and the stock came off the Wesson. He peered into the depths of the piece, and his frown became ferocious. When he looked up, Myron dreaded the message in his eyes.

'You've got a load of trash here, Duson,' he said. 'Marked trash, too. Why didn't you check to see where he kept the good stuff? You've wasted your time and my time, and you've got your heads in a noose in Texas. You idiots! I don't know why I waste my talents working with the likes of petty thieves like you! I'll have to get Simpson's bunch to fill the order, I suppose. And who else has such a lovely stock, just what the client wants?' He sighed and stalked from the bright garage back into the house and shut the door. The light went off and the garage doors went up.

Myron cleared his throat. 'Get the Wesson back in the van. We'll dump this lot in the first likely spot we see. Then we're goin' back and get rid of that woman. She's the only one can put us in Dutch, and we've got to get rid of her, permanent.'

3

The night was still dark and wet, but there was little traffic, and they made good time as they picked up Highway 171 again.

'We'll go down past De Ridder and turn back east on 196,' David Crowley said, studying the shining ribbon of road ahead of them. 'That'll put us back close, without having to travel far through Texas. Nobody will expect us to be heading back toward Templeton, anyway. We can get there in time to hide out until it's dark again. Then we can slip up and see what goes on at that house. I'll bet that woman is there by herself again.' His eyes gleamed, and he glanced down at the bite-mark on Duson's arm.

Myron growled deep in his throat and picked up speed. He had several good reasons now to want to put that woman down.

They went through Many very early in

the morning. Few cars were on the streets, and Myron took care to drive exactly at the speed limit, yet a cop-car turned a corner behind them and hit its lights. The siren wailed them to a stop.

The policeman looked sleepy and out of sorts. When Myron handed out his driver's license, the officer shone a flashlight back into the body of the van.

That woke him completely.

Duson saw the hand go for the gun, and he rolled over the engine housing, over the surprised Crowley's lap, and out the far door before the officer could even think about firing.

They had stopped alongside a closed service station, whose apron disappeared behind it into darkness broken only by the dim shapes of trees. Myron dashed for that cover, hearing a single set of footsteps following him. He pushed through a screen of bushes, and the footing went out from under him, letting him drop into dark space. He hit with a splash in knee-deep water, cold as a witch's tit, and another splash told him that one of his men had made it with him.

'Who is it?' he breathed.

'Frenchy,' came the reply. 'We move fas', my frien'. That cop, he call for backup. They be here any minute, an' we better be gone. I don' know thees place. They do. We cross, you theenk?' He was called Frenchy by all who knew him because of his thick Cajun accent, so thick you could cut it with a knife, some said.

Myron pushed up the muddy bank on the far side of the creek. There was a thick stand of pines there, and he went deep into it before it began to thin again, letting onto a quiet residential street. Cars were parked in the semidarkness between the light standards, and nothing moved except a prowling cat, which whisked across the street and into the shelter of an old-fashioned veranda.

'You give me one minute,' came Frenchy's quiet voice, 'an' I have one of these theeng go.'

He was as good as his word. Without a sound, the Cajun opened the door of a pale gray Mazda and slid under the steering wheel. A few deft motions of his fingers brought a cough, and the engine fired quietly enough not to wake the sleepers in the nearby houses.

Myron piled into the other side, and they crept away from the curb without turning on the lights. At the corner, Frenchy pulled the switch, and twin beams glared into the early-morning dimness. They stopped at the stop sign.

Three police cars were pulled up alongside the main street-cum-highway, and the van was surrounded by a swarm of uniformed men. Myron cursed softly as the Crowley twins were dragged out of the rear doors and bundled unceremoniously into a waiting squad car. None of what he saw did a thing to ease his mind or make him any happier. He had undertaken a job that should have been easy and profitable. But instead, it had all turned terribly wrong. Now he had lost his van and half his team was being hauled away where, no doubt, they would sing like canaries.

Myron Duson was as angry as he ever got — and when the big man lost his temper, it was time to go home and bar all the doors.

★ ★ ★

Lily lay flat on her back on the spool bed in which her grandmother had given birth to eight stillborn children, one daughter, and Lily's father. Her mother had died there, too, at the age of seventy-one, but none of that troubled her. Dying was about the only thing in her existence that, strangely, had never frightened Lily Frost.

Many other things terrified her, however; the worst being her former lover, Martin Fewell. She still had paralyzing nightmares in which Martin came bursting into this house, struck down her brother Stony, and dragged her away again into the abusive drug-ridden existence from which she had, with great effort, escaped.

When those four men had broken through the door and confronted her in the kitchen, she had been certain that they were led by her former lover and worst enemy. It had been pure desperation, she was certain, that had given her the courage to bite the man who grabbed her, setting her teeth into his hairy arm until she tasted blood. She hoped he would get tetanus from that bite — or even hydrophobia! She laughed silently to herself at the thought.

She had turned restlessly then, twisting the blanket and the handmade quilt around her body so tightly that she had to free herself and straighten the covers all out again. She stared at the dim glimmer of light from the yard lamp outside, which was reflected in her dresser mirror. The reflection looked as wet as the stormy night. A constant flap of drenched branches against the wooden siding of the house made her jump, her nerves jolting every time.

There was a light tap at the door, and she smiled faintly. That would be Stony, worried about her. 'Yes, come in,' she murmured, and the door opened to admit his slight shape.

He was carrying a teacup, which he balanced with great care, for his limp tended to slosh liquids. 'Here, I thought you might need this. I've got some sleeping stuff that the doctor gave me. Do you want that, too?'

She sat and pushed back the covers, swinging her long legs over the edge of the bed and reaching for her robe. 'No, thanks, Stony. Just the tea. That should relax me enough to let me sleep. You know I try not to take anything, now. Not anything at all. Something might react with the drugs and set things off again, when I'm finally getting on top of the flashbacks.'

He nodded as he backed up to sit in her small rocker. The fitful light, finding its way through swaying branches to her window, danced on his face, which seemed thinner and paler than ever after the evening's events. He looked entirely too frail, she realized, and the thought frightened her.

'Stony,' she said, reaching for the cup he had set on the dressing table, 'you ought to take something yourself. You look like a ghost. I'll be all right — I always am.' She shivered as she sipped at the hot tea, into which he had put a drop of their grandfather's brandy.

'Lily, we've got to talk. I wasn't able before, but you ought to know what's going to happen. If they put you on the witness stand when they catch those men, whoever defends them is going to tear you apart, trying to make it seem like you aren't a reliable witness. Have you thought about that?' He leaned forward, his hands tight on the curved arms of the rocker.

She sank onto the edge of the bed, warming her hands around the cup. She could see herself in the mirror, a dim ghost of a reflection with huge eyes that were wells of shadow. *More like me than I am in the daylight*, she thought.

She turned back to her brother. 'I know. I've . . . been on a witness stand before. I never told you, because I hate to remember it. That lawyer did it, too. He made me look like a crazy dope-ridden woman who couldn't understand what was going on, no matter what she thought she saw — and the jury believed it. That's why . . . ' She took a long draught of the tea, warming herself to the pit of her stomach against the memory. ' . . . that's one of the reasons I ran away and came home. They let Martin out, you see, and he knew I'd testified against him. He killed . . . but you don't want to know about that . . . and I don't want to remember it. He came after me, and I ran. I've been expecting him to come here to exact his revenge on me ever since.'

She gave a long shuddering sigh. 'When I thought it was Martin with those men, I knew there was no good reason for me being afraid anymore. They were going to kill me, and if I could make them sorry for what they'd done, I was going to do it. I wish — I wish I'd done the same thing to Martin a long time before he killed that kid. Things might have been different if I had.'

Stony was staring at her, his eyes wide and his face tense. 'I didn't know about all that, dear. I know it isn't going to be easy, but we'll be in this together. You're dead certain you can identify — but of course you are. I'll go away and let you sleep now.'

He rose stiffly and limped away down the hall, leaving her staring once again at the ceiling. This time, she was relaxed. The hot tea and the brandy had loosened her muscles — and her mind — and she knew she could sleep now.

But instead she chose to relive that old trial, the details of which she had thought lay forever lost in the fogs of the past . . .

★   ★   ★

'You saw this man, Martin Fewell, attack Samuel Barrett? With your own eyes? You were present at the struggle?' The defense counsel's hard gray eyes bored into hers, making her throat constrict.

'I was there, yes. And I saw Martin hit him with his fists. Then, when the boy got up again, he picked up a two-by-four and hit him over the head with it. He beat his head until the board sounded squishy when it hit.' There, it was out, and she hadn't faltered.

'But had you not taken drugs earlier in the evening? Mind-altering drugs, which often produce delusions in the minds of those who take them?' His gaze was intent, intimidating.

'Martin gave me those things, yes, but not on that day. I hadn't taken anything on that day — and I know what I saw. I saw Martin kill Sammy.' She felt tears starting in her eyes, and she sensed, also, Martin's angry glare from his seat at the defense table.

The lawyer leaned forward like a wolf about to go in for the kill. 'But is it not true that you sometimes have what's known as flashbacks, sudden episodes of disorientation caused by the drug, even when you haven't had any for some time?'

It was true. She nodded, wordless, and bent her head to stare into her lap. But that wasn't what happened! she cried inside herself. She knew it was hopeless . . . Martin was about to get away with murder.

Lily sighed softly. She had lived through all that and through the constant terror that Martin would search for her afterward. She could survive this, too. She closed her eyes and, miraculously, slept.

But among her restless dreams, a dim shape prowled, sometimes as Martin, sometimes as that other man who resembled him so closely. She sat again in that courtroom, but this time it was Stony whose death she remembered, and it was that other Martin who had killed him.

She forced herself out of the depths of her dream and sat up, her eyes wide, staring at the shadow of the branches on the wall. Fury built inside her, burning away at the residue of timidity that had troubled her for so long.

'Nobody's going to hurt my brother!' she whispered, clenching her long fingers into fists. 'I won't let anyone hurt my Stony!'

Somehow, that resolve eased her inner tensions. When she slept again, it was dreamless and sound.

* * *

The next morning was a difficult one for Livingston. The night before he had been so sick with worry about his sister, that he had given little thought to what had happened in his home. But now, in the newly washed sunlight, he could see the traces where those men had passed and done their damage. He felt as if their filthy hands had dirtied him as well.

The furniture, while scratched, was mostly undamaged, testifying to the staying power of solid Philippine mahogany. The antique ruby glass, of course, was irreparable, and Lily vacuumed the spot where it had been smashed to bits, after they picked up the curving shards with careful fingers. It took some time to get the house into order again, but even then it felt as if a secure stronghold had been breached. It would never be the same again.

The places on the walls where his showpieces once hung reminded him, when he looked up, that he had lost objects that he was truly fond of — even though their value was minimal. The Baby Dragoon Revolver that had been his grandfather's was one item that he wished, now, he had put into the bank. It had had extensive repair, but the old man had carried it for years, and it was the one gun Stony most wanted to keep. Now it was in the hands of thieves.

He shook the thought away and turned to stare around the big parlor. 'It feels as if somebody's ruined something important,' he mused.

Lily straightened and stared into his face, her eyes wide. 'Yes. That's the way Martin made me feel, all the time. I thought I was through with that, and here it comes again. Last night — Stony, I was scared out of my wits. But somehow I came through it. Out the other side, you know? After you left, I got hold of myself. I think things will be all right now.'

She was a bit pale, the bandage on her head making her look rather jaunty. She was polishing the big claw-footed table in the center of the room, rubbing it with lemon oil as if to remove the taint of those who had violated their space. Something else was troubling her, he could tell, but he would wait until she was ready to talk to him about it.

They moved the table back into the precise spot from which it had been pushed. They straightened the cut glass and porcelain and Majolica ware that had been displaced from the shelves in the corner of the room. Lily dusted everything carefully, wiping away all trace of the intruders and the fingerprint powder as well.

At last, she nodded to him. 'You sit down for a while. You look tired. I'll get us some coffee, and then I want to talk to you. I'm worried about something silly, and you can tell me I'm not as well as I pretend to be, and maybe I'll stop worrying. Then again, maybe I'll just keep right on but hold it in.'

This was the time. He had learned to take advantage of every opportunity she gave him to help her with her long struggle. He sat in the stuffed plush armchair that still held the imprint of his grandfather's ample bottom; he slipped down into the depression, as always, feeling himself ridiculously slight and frail, compared with the burly Scotsman who had put together the heritage of the Frosts. When Lily returned with the lacquered tray and two Haviland cups and saucers, the rose-sprigged pot, and the Irish linen napkins, he felt tears come to his eyes. That was the signal his mother had used whenever she had something of importance to discuss with his father. They had known as children to go about their own affairs, leaving the adults to solve whatever strange problems haunted their distant world.

When the cups were filled, the steam rising from the flared shapes, and the napkins were properly placed on their laps, Lily took a sip, as if for courage. Then she set her saucer carefully on the big table and leaned forward, resting her elbows on her knees in the old tomboyish way her mother had disliked so much.

'Stony, I had a dream.'

'I suspect we both had bad dreams last night, Lily. I tossed and turned all night — except when I was having nightmares.' He knew this wasn't what she meant, and he waited for her to continue.

'It wasn't that sort of dream, Stony. I've had them before — dreamed things that really happened later. But sometimes, if I realized what it was — what might happen — I have done things differently.

And it's meant that things turned out in a different way. I don't know — am I making it clear?'

'You mean that you dreamed something bad would happen, changed what you were going to do because of the dream — and nothing bad came afterward,' he said. He didn't mention it, but he had done something of the sort himself.

'Yes. I dreamed that Martin was going to kill me, the night before he killed that boy. So the next morning I got up and went out early to the grocery store. When I got back, he was already after Sammy, and he killed him while I watched. The neighbors came before he could get at me, too.' She looked rather defiant, as if she expected him to laugh at the notion.

'So what was it you dreamed this time that frightened you so much?' he asked in his gentlest tone.

'I dreamed that either Martin, or that man who looked like him, killed *you*. And I have the strongest feeling that if we don't understand that can happen . . . we may regret it terribly. I want you to take

58

this whole thing seriously, Stony. I want you to carry a weapon on you all the time. What have you got that you can carry without it seeming to be a weapon? It seems as if Grandfather had something sneaky, but I can't quite remember what it was.'

Livingston felt a strange sensation go through him, half-recognition and half-comfort. Lily cared about him and worried about him. He'd wondered, as she worked through her long time of trauma, if she had time even to think of him at all. Now he knew that she did.

'The rifle cane,' he said after thinking about it for a minute. 'Grandfather bought it in 1910 from a bankrupt estate over in Louisiana. Single shot, rim fire, .32 caliber, grip shaped like the head of a dog. It looks like a walking stick, but it contains one round that can come as a very nasty surprise to anyone expecting to find a . . . helpless cripple who can't defend himself.'

'Yes!' she said, leaning even farther in her chair. 'I remember now; Gramma found me playing with it in their closet once, and took me out right then, loaded it, and made me fire it at the ash barrel. I'll never forget the cloud of ashes that flew in all directions when the slug hit the barrel. Then she hid it away, and I barely remembered enough about it to bring it to mind. That's what you need, Stony. It wasn't displayed in the house — I'd remember if it had been.'

'It's in my closet. For some reason, I always liked the thing — it reminded me of Grandfather. It's behind my garment bag, on the left side, if you want to go up and get it. We'll load it right now, if that'll make you happier.' He found himself strangely excited at the thought of carrying the cane, which would never be recognized for what it was except by another expert in antique firearms.

She was gone at once, and he heard her impatient steps crossing the landing, going up the second flight of steps, pattering down the worn carpet of the second-floor hallway. He leaned back in the worn chair and looked at the ceiling, where two linked rings of discoloration had formed when the roof had leaked once when he was a child. The spot still reminded him of the youngster he used to be.

This old house was sound. He had taken care of that, but he hadn't redone much of anything. He didn't care for modern things, and Lily seemed not to mind. But perhaps he should have the roof checked again before the next rainy season. It seemed to him, staring at the space above his head, that the circles had a damp spot in the center of each.

The footsteps came tripping down the stairs again; Lily entered the parlor, holding the rifle cane carefully in both hands. The gutta percha that formed it was a bit dusty, and she wiped it with her dust cloth before handing it to him.

Livingston twisted the dog's-head grip, unlocking the mechanism from the cane's barrel. He pressed the latch, letting the spring zip forward. He blew the dust out and squeezed the grip, pulling the spring back into place, where he locked it with the latch again. The barrel was also dusty. He sent Lily for his gun-cleaning kit and pulled the swab through by the tough string. When he looked inside, the interior was shiny once more.

The mechanism was so simple that there was nothing else to do except to load the thing. There were cartridges of all calibers in the breakfront, along with his loading equipment. Once the .32 cartridge was in place, and the stock relocked onto the barrel, the cane became once again a respectable gentleman's support, never betraying its deadly contents. The weight was just right — not too much for a cane that could be carried comfortably.

He rose, using it as a support, and moved around the room. 'I don't know why I haven't used this before now,' he said, tapping briskly around the big table. 'It's just the right length, and I could use it for a sort of trademark. It's old enough not to come under the Firearms Act, too, so I shouldn't be in too much trouble if I got caught with it.'

'Wash wouldn't care,' Lily said. She looked more relaxed now.

'I travel a lot. But when I travel, I'm not likely to meet either Martin or his lookalike. So if I use it here at home, taking it with me for display, then I suspect it'll work out rather well.' He smiled at her, feeling an unaccustomed tenderness. They had lived together without quarreling, but without overt affection for so long, that it took him a while to realize what he felt was a remnant of that old childhood love they had shared. 'We're both crippled, you know?' he mused aloud. His own voice startled him, and he glanced up at Lily, afraid that he might have wounded her.

But she was nodding. 'You're right. I've been crippled in my mind, you in your body, and we've been trying so hard not to show it that we haven't had the time to take care of each other properly. But I think that's changed, Stony. Maybe those nasty men did us a favor. We needed a shock, something harsh and painful, to wake us up. And now that we're awake, let's not go back to sleep. I want to keep alert, because that big man reminded me too much of Martin. I believe Martin would come back and kill me if he thought he could get away with it. You really didn't know him, but I knew him entirely too well. I want to sleep with one eye open for a while.'

Livingston had been trying to ignore his own intuition. He, too, had a feeling that the problem was far from over. 'Why don't I call Shipp and see what they've discovered?' he asked, pulling himself up and balancing on the cane.

When Shipp's assistant, Lucy Fowler, answered, Stony was assaulted with questions. 'Yes, we're both all right. No problem. I just wanted to find out if Shipp knows anything yet. They did find those fingerprints, and there should have been time to get word about the FBI files on them.'

Lucy, of course, knew everything that the sheriff knew. 'The word came in about a half hour ago,' she said. 'Sheriff Shipp was going to come out and talk with you and your sister, but he was called away to an unrelated accident. I can get it the report — yes, here it is, on the computer. The prints they found are those of Donald Crowley, white male, twenty-seven years of age, convicted in St.

Tammany Parish five years ago of armed robbery, rape, and homicide in connection with the holdup of a convenience store and the capture of a hostage. One nasty customer, Stony.'

'How in hell did he get out of prison so soon?' Livingston felt a helpless rage building in his chest. 'With all those convictions, he should have been put away for good.'

She sighed audibly. 'You know how it goes. They appealed, and the appellate court found a tiny technical flaw in the first trial. A misplaced comma or something just as ridiculous. So they turned him loose, and now he's at it again. His twin, David, is just as bad a piece of work, but he's never been convicted yet.'

'Is there any information that might lead to the others? That big man that looked like Martin Fewell, for instance.'

He heard keys tapping. Then, 'In prison, Crowley was boon companions with a fellow called Myron Duson. His people came from Louisiana, but he has kin all over southern Texas as well. He was in for extortion with the threat of violence. The picture they faxed to us looks quite a lot like Martin Fewell. They know, Wash said, that this man's been into a lot of things, from dope to prostitution to grand larceny, but he's been too slick to get sent up for more than a couple of years at a time. And he got out early the last time for good behavior, if you can believe that.' She paused and cleared her throat. When she spoke again, it was carefully, as if she didn't want to alarm him. 'His M.O. is very simple, actually. He tries never to leave a witness alive to identify him.'

'Damn!' Livingston found that he was gripping the phone with a hand suddenly damp with sweat. 'I had the feeling — Lucy, I think Lily's in a lot of danger. What should we do?'

'I'm not the lawman around here, Stony. I just don't know. But when Wash gets back, I'll have him call or come out and talk to you both. We can't have you and your sister living in fear. If you need to leave the house for a while, do you have someplace to go?'

Livingston thought for a long moment. The only possibility was not one he fancied. 'Well, yes, Lucy. But I'd like to put that off as long as possible. And I'd like for it to be kept secret, even from you and the deputies, if you don't mind, so I won't mention where it is. You tell Wash to call. And thanks.'

He turned from the phone, leaning against the breakfront. He felt suddenly dizzy, and Lily came to his side, concern on her face. 'You okay?' she asked, helping him sit again in the oversized chair.

He managed a grin. 'Of course. Just too much excitement, I think. Shipp will be out, probably late. We'll talk over what we need to do when he gets here, all right? I'm just not up to it right now.'

To his relief, she nodded and went back to her polishing. There was no need to worry her more than she was already. But that left Stony to worry alone.

4

Wash got to his office early the next morning after getting the first official input on the descriptions of the men who had robbed the Frost home. He hadn't slept well, because he couldn't stop thinking about the brutal attack on Lily Frost and the bold theft of her brother's guns. Both thoughts filled him with a sense of foreboding.

He was glad he hadn't thrown that earlier interstate report away. He dug it out of the desk drawer where he had put it and read it over again, this time looking for possible clues. This almost had to be the same bunch mentioned there, the Duson gang, and he hated to think of those thugs operating in his territory. The further fact that the leader of the gang, Myron Duson, had once bragged he never left a witness alive if he could help it, was particularly troubling to Shipp. Ironically, Duson had had only one major conviction, and had served very little jail time apparently because of his uncanny ability to avoid eye-witness identification. Given all that, Shipp was convinced there was a very good possibility that Duson, at least, might try to come back to Templeton in order to silence Lily.

Poor Lily, Wash mused. Life had certainly dealt her a pretty bad hand, beginning with that scoundrel Martin Fewell. The Fewells had lived on a hard-scrabble plot down near the Nichayac, back when Wash used to visit his grandparents on their farm deep in the riverbottom country. His Aunt Libby knew Mrs. Fewell, as they were both devoted gardeners, but she carefully avoided talking about the old man, Martin's father.

'They's religious folks and they's mean folks,' she had told Wash's mother once, shaking her head in disgust. 'But when you get both kinds of those kinds of folks together in one skin, you've got a *really* nasty kind of person.'

Wash, quiet as usual, and listening with both ears wide open, had found himself wondering how religious people could be mean, but he knew better than to open his mouth when the big folks were talking.

When he was quiet as a church mouse in the corner, grown folks tended to forget he was there at all. He learned quite a few of his life lessons that way.

'Well, ol' Mr. Fewell sure is religious,' his mother replied. 'And he seems to be particularly mean as well. I was down that way just the other day and met Miz Fewell walkin' along the road. She had bruises all down her arms and her face was a sight to see. Said she'd fell down the porch steps, but I know the shape of a fist-bruise when I see it. That ol' man'd been beatin' on her again is my guess.'

Aunt Libby nodded solemnly.

'The children say he knocks his young 'uns 'round all the time. The girls are afeared to talk about it, but young Marty, he talks a mite too much. They say he cusses his old man so as to make a sailor blush.'

Unseen, Wash had nodded agreement. He had heard all that himself. He knew he ought to feel sorry for a boy whose Pap beat him like that — but somehow he couldn't. Martin seemed to be just about as mean as his daddy was, and he was tough as a *bois d'arc* root. Everyone knew Martin Fewell would hit any other child he could reach — and then lied about it with a straight face if the kid complained to the teacher or his parents.

So Wash Shipp had avoided Martin like the plague all his life, and even now, as a lawman, he found himself frowning with dislike, just thinking about him. But according to Lily's own testimony, the attacker *hadn't* been Martin Fewell! He just looked like him. With all the descriptions and the one fingerprint they found, surely he could get a positive I.D. on that one.

And even as he sat there contemplating that possibility, Amy brought in a new printout. 'We've got a fingerprint identification,' she said. 'Belongs to an ex-con named Crowley. What's more, he's a known associate of Myron Duson, the one they mentioned in those dispatches you were going over yesterday. What do you want to bet they figured out this particular scam while they were in stir together?'

'That's as good a guess as any, Amy,' Wash said, studying the new report. 'But at this point it's just that, a good guess. We'll need to put together more of the puzzle before we wind up our springs and go off into orbit.'

He placed the new printout in the growing Frost file, along with his notes from the scene and the description report.

'It's a damned good start though,' he said, turning to the other accumulations piling up on his desk. 'It's a pretty damned good start.'

It was going to be another long day for the Sheriff of Nichayac County.

* * *

Over a span of twenty years, Martin Fewell had gotten old. He wasn't particularly old in years — but physically and mentally he had deteriorated a lot. His craggy face was riddled with wrinkles caked with what seemed to be centuries-old dust, and his hair, once as shiny black as a raven's wing, had turned a nondescript brownish-gray. His husky frame, which had allowed him to manhandle and mistreat Lily and all the others over the years, had shrunk back on his bones, leaving his spine painfully gnarled and humped and his skin hanging loosely at neck and belly.

And Martin felt as old as Methuselah, he often thought as he made his erratic way from town to town in the ten-year-old Chevy pickup that he hoped would last forever. Keeping the truck running and finding food to eat kept him strapped for cash and working at penny-ante jobs in order to survive.

No longer did sheriffs and police chiefs automatically give him his walking papers when he came through town to post bills advertising the circus that was his present employer. He didn't look threatening to them anymore, just dingy and down-at-heel. He sometimes studied his image in the cracked mirror of whatever motel he had garnered for the night and felt nothing but a cold sense of emptiness where his old macho aggressiveness once had flourished. And during these moments of introspection, Martin Fewell often wondered what had become of Lily Frost.

When he was sober and in a good mood, he had always known that she was the best thing he ever had going for him. Her attempts at gentleness, her sacrifices to keep him well-fed and clothed, and her pathetic need for something stable in their lives had often annoyed him. Now he knew that he would give anything to undo the terrible series of actions that had turned her against him at last.

He sighed as he stepped down from the pickup and took out the posters he must put up that day. Being the advance man for the circus could have been interesting work for some, but for him, it was little more than a tedious, if necessary, chore — something to be gotten through as quickly and efficiently as possible. And now, just as he held the colorful poster against a tree and readied his staple gun, here came a stupid cop, gesturing for him to cease what he was doing.

'Something wrong, Officer?' he asked. 'The permits should have been arranged a week ago. Carroll Brothers Circus and Carnival.'

'We'll check,' the man said, taking him by the elbow and waltzing him toward the storefront housing the city hall. 'You just come with me.'

Damn! Martin thought. *You watch — those bastards probably forgot the permits, and now I'll have to pay a fine and this will be another job gone into la-la-land.*

He sat in an uncomfortable chair shaped like a washtub while the policeman went into the back room. There were few others there, and he could hear a radio droning the news in the adjoining city police office.

A name of a town caught his attention. ' . . . men apprehended at five o'clock a.m. are suspected to be those wanted in a burglary and assault last evening near Templeton, Texas. Two others escaped into the darkness and their trail has not yet been found. It is thought that a stolen car, found abandoned later beside Highway 171, may have been used in avoiding arrest.

'The collection of Livingston Frost, noted dealer in antique firearms, was taken in the robbery, and his sister was injured. There is an all-points bulletin out in eastern Texas and western Louisiana for those suspects not yet apprehended. One suspect is tentatively identified as Myron Duson, present address unknown. His companion is still unknown, though he is described as being tall, heavy-set, and wearing a hat with a wide brim, which hides his face.

'Another robbery has been reported in Many, Louisiana, this one involving two teenagers armed with switch-blades . . . '

Martin switched off his ears. Livingston Frost — his sister had to be his Lily. And her brother had been a wimpy little cripple. Could he be a gun dealer? Antique guns? Probably. It was the sort of easy business a man like that might get into, though the subject of her brother's business had never come up during his time with Lily.

As he sat thinking, the officer returned. 'No permits have been obtained,' he said, his tone brusque. 'Sorry, Mr. Fewell, but you'll have to leave your posters unposted. There's no fine, as you hadn't put one up, but I'd suggest you move on. Granger isn't a good town for folks like you.'

Martin nodded and went back out to his truck. He'd never seen a hick town that was a good one for him. He could say that he was an expert on the insides of shabby jails and the wrong sides of redneck police and deputies who were long on muscle and short on brains.

The cop had followed him onto the street, and he turned to the officer suddenly and said, 'Could you tell me how far it is to Templeton, Texas?'

The man looked puzzled for a moment. Then his face brightened. 'Oh, yeah. Little town on the Nichayac River. I don't know in miles, but I figure about four and a half hours — driving the speed limit.'

Martin tried to smile at the cop's subtle attempt at humor. 'Thanks, Boss. Got some folks over there, and I think I'll pay 'em a visit.'

As he pulled away, the old truck rattling and groaning, the cop was still standing there, staring after him. Martin thanked his luck that it had been some years since his assault trial and all that bad publicity that had followed him when he'd been turned loose. These country cops could figure out ways to lock you up that would boggle the mind.

He turned west on Interstate 10. Lily didn't want to see him, he knew, but he had suddenly realized that he needed to see her. He needed to say something to her.

Maybe he just needed to tell her he was sorry. Not only for what he had done to her — but for what others like him had done as well.

★   ★   ★

Allison Frost Vernier, in spite of her advanced age, was still going strong. She had married late in life, and after taking that drastic step, she had been so absorbed in getting her house (and her somewhat bewildered husband) into order that she lost touch with her kinfolk in Templeton. Their father had been her nephew, which made them somewhat distant both in age and consanguinity, and that made it easy for them to slip out of her immediate ken.

So when the phone rang, early on a rainy morning in late March, she expected it to be one of her many acquaintances who shared her passion for breeding registered English setters. But it was her great-nephew, Livingston Frost. His voice was one she recognized only after some thought, for she missed his first words, her hearing not being as accurate as she pretended.

'Who?' She shook the receiver, as if that might clear up the tinny stream of words.

Again he spoke. 'Aunt Allie, it's Livingston. Stony. You remember me — my grandfather was your brother. My sister Lily and I haven't seen you in years, but surely you remember us!'

She detected in his voice something too much like desperation to be comfortable.

'Of course I remember. I'm not senile, Livingston, whatever anyone might say. And what might I do for you?'

She was hoping devoutly that this was just an idle chat, for she drove herself and everyone on her large farm with an intensity that brooked no interruptions. She was always frantically busy and had little time for socializing, kin or no kin.

'We need . . . we need a place to hide, Aunt Allie.'

She shook the phone again. Surely he'd said he needed a place to hide, and that simply could not be correct. 'Repeat that. I thought I heard you say — '

'That I need to hide. Yes. Or rather, Lily needs to. We were robbed, and the ringleader of the criminals has a reputation of never leaving a witness alive. And Lily saw him and can identify him. Aunt Allie, we've got to find someplace where he can't find us. Just for a while. Will Uncle Louis mind?'

Had it really been that long? She sighed. 'Your Uncle Louis died two years ago, Livingston. And if you need a refuge, of course you can stay with me. I hope you don't mind working in the kennels a bit — we're short-handed right now, and extra help would be a godsend. Is Lily . . . ' She paused, trying to think of a tactful way to ask the question. ' . . . is Lily feeling up to helping out, too?'

His voice reassured her. 'Lily's pulled out of her problem almost completely. That's why I need to get her out of harm's way, so none of this new mess can send her into a tailspin. She works like a Trojan. Keeps house and cooks for me, and works in the garden. She can help too, Aunt Allie. I'm the one who has a bit of trouble getting around.'

'Oh, yes. The polio. I keep forgetting. Nevertheless, you must both come to me at once. If someone's threatening to kill my niece, we must hide her well and protect her intelligently. I won't brook anyone threatening my family, no matter what. Bring some of your guns, Stony. All I have is a twenty-gauge shotgun loaded with birdshot and a .38 pistol.'

Already her busy mind was arranging rooms, laying out plans to keep both of her kinfolk occupied enough to avoid thinking about their situation. The dogs were important to her, but she had never become so attached to them that she valued them above people.

'We can come tomorrow, if that's all right?' Stony sounded relieved.

'Come at once, if you want. Can't have my niece murdered by a burglar, now can we?' She stretched her arthritic knee and set about flexing it, ignoring the pain as she kept it mobile. 'You come right on, and I'll have things ready when you arrive.'

'Thanks, Auntie. And I'm sorry about Uncle Louis. I didn't know.' He sounded genuinely regretful.

'My own fault, boy. I should have written you, but somehow, what with the estate and the dogs and everything, I never even wrote his own sister down in Lafayette. I'll do that right now, before I forget again.'

She wrote the note before rising from the telephone table, scribbling an abrupt and yet heartfelt message inside a notecard and stamping it for mailing. But her mind was not entirely on her task. She was thinking of her niece, Lily, who once had been a drug addict and a runaway. The child had been dreamy and hard to handle, it was true. But Allison felt rather certain that her great-niece's adventure in her youth had been caused by the sort of romantic nature she recognized in herself. Her own marriage had been as unexpected and intense, as shocking to those who knew her as a reclusive and intellectual thirty-year-old, as Lily's abrupt departure had been to her immediate family. Only a matter of generations had made a difference in the way that trait had cropped out.

She rose, forcing her back straight, and made her recalcitrant knees march toward the kitchen, where her friend and long-time employee now reigned. 'Maggie,' she called as she stumped into the room, 'we're going to have company. My brother's grandchildren are coming for a visit.'

Not for a moment did she consider letting Maggie know the reason for that visit. The girl had, at seventy-two, settled down a bit, but she still was prone to excited ditherings over what had to be taken as the normal dangers and dilemmas of life.

'The little boy and girl? Miss Allie! What a treat! They must be grown by now.' Maggie's coffee-colored cheeks stretched into a grin.

'And then some,' Allison said, her tone gruff. 'Tell Sissy to make up the two front rooms over the south porch. Livingston is lame — you remember he had polio, back when he was a child? So see that the little stair-rail lift is working, to take him up the stairs.'

Maggie looked smug. 'Been wanting to fix it up so's you can use it your own self,' she mumbled toward the piecrust she was rolling paper-thin on the marble slab topping the work table.

Allison was not that deaf. 'I heard that! The day I'm too lame to climb my own stairs, I shall move my bedroom down into the sun parlor and forget the house has those upstairs rooms. Until then, you just do as I ask and don't try to make me feel old!'

* * *

The day whisked past, and by the time the Toyota pulled to a stop in the drive, everything had been done to her specifications, although she had spent most of that period exercising the dogs. Her staff, rare in these modern times, was middle-aged to elderly, determined to last at least as long as she did, and devoted to their crotchety employer. Things got done at Allison Vernier's breeding farm, and others in the business could only envy her.

She showered and changed. When the newcomers stepped out of the little car, she went slowly down the steps to meet them, her gait nicely suited to the condition of her knees. 'Stony! Lily!' She stretched out her hands to them, noting with unexpected pain that both now showed their age, and detecting the effort with which her great-nephew forced his thin limbs to move as he came to meet her.

'Aunt Allie.' He took her hand lightly into his, and she realized that he, too, knew the agony of a tight handclasp on meeting a stranger unfamiliar with arthritic joints.

Lily stood there, tall and lanky, her expression uncertain. Though she was every day of thirty-nine, she still had the look of an awkward teenager. Allison put an arm about her waist (being too short to reach any higher) and gave her a little hug.

'Welcome, children. It's been too long — and we're the last of the Frosts. We must do this more often and with happier reasons.' She reached to take her cane from the spot where she had leaned it against the porch railing, and they moved together back into the house.

It was strange, she thought as she ushered them into the sitting room and placed them on either side of her deep chair. She had all but forgotten these two in her busy round of tasks. Yet now that she saw them, she felt a surge of protective possessiveness go through her. They were her own flesh and blood, her brother's descendants. Anyone threatening them would have Allison Frost Vernier to contend with!

But she made herself relax, smiling and chatting and helping her guests to lose a bit of the tension that was so evident in their bodies and faces. By the time Maggie came with coffee in the best china cups and plates of thin teacakes, they had all begun to talk easily together in the faded splendor of the sitting room, with the last of the sunset dyeing the sky scarlet beyond the French windows.

While Livingston described the burglary, she watched Lily. According to her infrequent communications with Livingston, the girl had been extremely frightened and terribly passive after her return home. Allison felt certain she had been desperately mistreated by the man with whom she eloped. That had, to an extent, disgusted her, for she felt that any Frost worth her salt would have left the son-of-a-bitch, or killed him, or both.

But now Lily seemed reasonably relaxed. She even described the men who broke into the house, though in years past she would have left all the talking to her brother. Her eyes had lost the look of fear that had lived there for so long, though by rights this new danger should have left her terrified.

Allison found herself growing angry. What right had a bunch of toughs to come pushing in and interrupt the ongoing recovery of this precious niece of hers, who had survived so much pain and turmoil?

'Did you bring any of your guns?' she asked Stony when Lily was done. 'I called the sheriff after we talked, and he said he'd do what he could, but this is a poor parish, and he hasn't enough deputies to set up a round-the-clock guard or anything like that.'

'The thieves got all the ones at the house,' Stony said, 'and I sold all the ones I took to the show. I didn't think we should take the extra time to get anything out of the bank vault, but I brought this one with me — it isn't much good for an extended fire-fight, but it could surprise the heck out of one person, one time.'

He offered her his cane, and she chuckled as she recognized her brother's the old piece. 'Good thinking. I wish I had one of these myself. You just use keep on using that cane as if it were nothing but a walking stick, and I'll load my .38 — you remember it, Stony? — and I'll keep it in my pocket. We'll shock the hell out of anybody who thinks he's going to run over us!'

Somewhat to her surprise, Allison felt an unaccustomed surge of exhilaration. It had been a long time since she had been faced with any kind of danger, and she felt her blood warming, and her heartbeat picking up its pace.

Not since that long-ago feud with the political bosses running her parish had she needed to gear up for war, and it amused her to find that she was no more civilized now than she had been forty years ago.

5

In spite of his frequent brushes with the law, Étienne Carrefours, better known as Frenchy to his friends and associates, was not a wicked man. He had always assured himself that he was simply a thief — the best in the business, mind you — but not an example that the old *mamères* would use to frighten the children.

But now he was growing more and more uncomfortable.

Myron Duson, to all intents and purposes, *was* a violent man; there was no getting around that fact. He had the reputation for being one who left no living witnesses, though Frenchy had discounted that when he first was told that about Myron. Surely nobody would be so foolish as to kill, take a human life, without it being a case of life or death?

But this first job with Duson had shaken Frenchy's confidence. Duson had a flair for larceny — that fact was undeniable. Yet this particular job, which should have been a no-brainer, had gone sour from the moment they walked into that old house in east Texas and discovered the skinny woman making bread in the kitchen.

Frenchy had a weakness for tall slender women, and he particularly liked the ones who showed domestic talents. He had been secretly relieved when it turned out that David Crowley hadn't bashed in the lady's skull after all. Then, when he discovered that the so-called 'priceless' guns they had stolen were almost worthless, it had filled him with a sort of wry amusement. Duson was so damned cocksure, so domineering, and so harsh that this proof of his fallibility was something Frenchy could savor. Nobody was as good as Myron thought he was!

And at that moment, Frenchy had been ready to bail out of the deal and go his own way. A thief with his expertise was always in demand, and he didn't have to stand, like a stubborn mule, hitched up with this man who seemed, more and more, to be crazy.

And this new decision of Duson's was a proof of that.

The two of them, after watching the Crowley twins hauled off, had gotten clean away from that disaster. Why wasn't Duson heading for the tall timber now? Anyone with half an ounce of sense would have done just that. But no! Duson was headed *back* to east Texas to try to kill that woman again!

Which was way too risky and made no sense at all to Frenchy. He wanted very badly to stop the car, get out, and walk away across the flat fields alongside Interstate 10. He was certain, however, that if he tried doing that, Duson would pull out his gun and shoot him squarely in the back. And whatever else he might think or believe, Frenchy Carrefours had no desire to die for no good cause. Life was good, and his *jolie catin*, his pretty woman, Marie, still waited patiently for him in the little town, in Calcasieu Parish where their Acadian ancestors had settled after fleeing Canada. '*Laissez les bons temps rouler* — Let the good times roll!' had always been Frenchy's motto . . . and he wasn't about to do a change up now.

He fondly thought of Marie, his *'tit peau de chou*, his 'little sweet potato,' as the Cajuns said. Something about that skinny woman Duson was so determined to kill reminded him of her. Perhaps that was why his spirit just wasn't in the present job in hand. And it was yet another good reason to slip away from this madman while he had the chance and make a beeline back to Cajun country.

As Frenchy continued driving . . . and reflecting on his odds of ditching the crazy man . . . Duson stared straight ahead, sleepless and wordless beside him. Shackled together like members of a chain gang, the reluctant partners were making their way back to Texas from Alexandria, Louisiana, way up in Caddo Parish, where they had retrieved traveling money from the secret stash Duson had hidden there.

But Duson was planning — what? — and why? Frenchy would have given a lot right then to know just what was going on behind those flat, cold reptile-like eyes.

He knew he was going to have to tread carefully going forward if he was going to survive this situation with his skin intact. And his first step would be to disable the car.

They had been stopping along the way, from time to time, for gas and food and to use the restrooms. Frenchy, an automotive genius, had always been meticulous about checking the oil in any car he drove, owned or stolen. He had witnessed too many careful planners brought down by a lack of attention to such seemingly minor details. They were in their fourth stolen car since that first one in which they had escaped the capture of the van and the arrest of the Crowley twins. This one was an unobtrusive gray Olds — an eighty-nine model, old enough not to arouse too much attention, and yet still powerful and reliable enough. Frenchy genuinely hoped its former driver had survived the crack on the head Duson had delivered unnecessarily when they had liberated the car back in Alexandria. As was his usual habit, Frenchy had developed a kind of affection for the old vehicle, as it purred along the Interstate to Lake Charles, turned toward DeRidder on Highway 171, and sped northward.

When they were far from any convenient source of stolen cars, he began to put his plan in to effect. The gas was getting low, just as he had intended. 'We mus' stop at the nex' Mom-and-Pop,' he said, his tone casual. 'We need gas, and I got to stretch or I be goin' to get too stiff for anythin'.'

Duson just grunted assent. He had been dozing restlessly for the past half-hour, and Frenchy hoped the big man had no suspicion that his reluctant henchman was getting restless.

'How 'bout I stop at Ragley. Li'l place up ahead,' Frenchy continued. 'Get plenty travelers t'rough dere, so they won' notice us, I think. You stay in de car, jus' in case . . . right dere, y'know, dere be a state road, turn off toward the wes' . . . save us gas and dere ought to be no cops dere at all. Nothin' out dere but pine tree for miles.' He glanced aside at Duson.

'Sounds good,' Duson said. 'Just do it and get on with it. The sooner we get that bitch quieted down for good, the sooner we can go about our business. Just let me sleep!' He hitched himself around, pulled his hat over his face, and went silent.

Just right, Frenchy thought. *You go on back to sleep, big man, and pay no mind to me.*

If the car happened to go dead somewhere between Ragley and Merriville, there'd be nothing to steal for miles, maybe. With any luck, Duson would get rattled enough to give him a chance to slip away into the woods; and once among the pines, Frenchy Carrefours could not be caught by any man — not unless he wanted to be.

★ ★ ★

Ragley consisted of one store and a sign pointing toward the state road to Merriville. Frenchy pulled to a stop beside the gas pumps and got out to stretch.

Duson didn't move, and a muffled

snort told him that the madman was still sleeping.

A cheerful-looking old fellow came out of the store, accompanied by the tinkle of an old-fashioned bell over the door, and asked, 'What kin I do for you?'

'Fill up de gas, will you, while I check de oil?'

Frenchy pulled the latch and moved to the front to open the hood. While nosing around in there, he quietly slit the oil line, punching a carefully gauged hole that would let the oil escape slowly enough to allow them to travel a certain distance. When the tank was filled, he put the hood down with a soft *thunk*, so as not to wake his passenger, and doled out a few bills into the old man's eager hand. The old fellow didn't notice a thing.

With a nod, Frenchy climbed back into the car and cranked it carefully — Duson would not hesitate to confiscate the ancient pickup truck parked at the side of the store building if the car showed any telltale signs of demise. The man had never learned anything about cars, and, to Frenchy, that was an ignorance that was about to cost him dearly.

He turned back onto the road. To his surprise, it had been blacktopped since he'd last driven in that direction. That would mean a bit more traffic than he remembered, but since he intended to leave this vehicle before they hit the next town of Merriville, it would probably make no difference to his overall plan.

* * *

It didn't take long to pass by all the houses strung loosely along the road leading out of Ragley. Then they were in pine timber country. Cut over time after time, the young trees were coming back strongly, and he smelled the familiar pine-straw scent with pleasure. It was spring! The woods were beginning to leaf out, the stands of hardwoods showed a mist of green, and the dogwoods were gleaming with fresh white blossoms among the dark tree trunks. It should be no problem to make his way by foot to a suitable highway, going as straight through the woods as any arrow, guided by his sure instinct for direction.

The miles passed, and he almost dozed himself, for the road was contained between walls of trees, without any break to make for interest. And then a deer darted from the hedgerow on the right, directly in front of the car.

Frenchy jammed on the brakes, sending Duson flopping onto the dash, his head thumping on the windshield. 'You damn fool! You tryin' to kill me?'

Duson was rubbing his head, looking about with the dazed expression a sudden awakening brings to a sleeper. 'Better you bump your head than bash our radiator on a deer!'

Frenchy pointed off to the left, where a blur of brown and a pale scut were rapidly disappearing into the trees. 'Well, start the goddam car and get us out of here!'

Naturally, the engine had died, much to Frenchy's satisfaction. The oil gauge, which had been indicating trouble for miles now, had died with the engine. When he tried the ignition, nothing happened — the thing was probably frozen up tight.

'What's the problem?' Duson opened his door and went around to the hood.

Frenchy smiled as he pulled the latch. Duson was so stupid he probably wouldn't notice anything less than an engine that was entirely missing. 'Let's see,' he said.

Standing beside his partner in crime, Frenchy bent over to peer into the workings of the motor. Oil was spattered all over everything, stinking to high heaven, but of course Duson didn't know that such a condition wasn't normal.

'I can't tell you. I see nothin' wrong, but this, it's a car I don' know. Maybe there was somethin' wrong when we take her, eh? It finally come apart and leave us stranded here. Miles from anyplace!' He managed to make his voice sound despairing.

'Where's the nearest town?'

Duson sounded ready to kill, and Frenchy stepped back. 'Maybe five, six mile. Not too far to walk. I do it many time back home.'

He knew with wicked amusement that Duson thought feet were made for the purpose of displaying expensive shoes. The idea of walking more than a couple of blocks would turn him pale. And it did.

'Six miles?' The man's tone was furious. 'Frenchy, when I told you to steal a car that wouldn't be noticeable, I thought you knew enough not to lift a junker. Six miles!' He turned back the way they had come. 'How far back to Ragley?'

'Ten mile, maybe.'

'Did we pass any farms along the way?'

'Nothin' but the pine tree for a long time now.'

'Shit!'

It was all the Cajun could do to keep from grinning openly. But instead he said, 'Maybe there be a house up ahead a little way. We gettin' closer to de nex' town than you think. You want to go see while I check out dis car? Maybe I can fin' what's wrong while you go.'

Muttering something obscene, Duson trudged away up the road without answering. If there was a house up ahead, Frenchy pitied anyone living there. The mood Duson was in, he would have pitied

101

a bear or a panther that met him on the road.

But that was not his concern right now. He would have time to get well into the woods before the madman returned; and, Frenchy bet, Myron Duson in the woods would be even more inept than he was under the hood of a car.

The Cajun waited until a long curve up ahead took the departing shape out of sight. Then Frenchy reached into the car for the bag of candybars he always carried when he traveled. This was wet country, and he'd find water, he knew, though he also knew that it wouldn't be that long before he emerged onto some road that would supply a ride or a vulnerable car to take him back toward Vinton and his waiting Marie.

Before Duson had gone a mile, the Cajun was strolling through a stand of young pine on the south side of the road. In another twenty minutes, he risked a snatch of song.

He was free of Duson at last!

His feet covered miles of pine plantings, as he thought with wicked glee about Duson's future. *Serve him right*, he thought, *if that lady there in Templeton kill him dead!*

But that was no longer any of his concern. He began whistling a favorite Zydeco tune, *Ma 'tit fille*, one he and Marie had danced to at the local dance hall. He was thinking about his future and the near miss he'd had with that *merde*, Myron Duson.

Maybe it was a sign. He wasn't getting any younger now. Could be it was time to cash in his chips and find a real job. But with the ins and outs of jail time, he wasn't a great risk. He wondered if he could pull together some seed money, and find a little cabin and piece of land out near one of the rivers. If he had a good sound *pirogue*, he could put up signs around town — maybe start a business taking out tourists.

Marie was a good, sound country girl. She knew how to make ends meet. Together, he knew, they could make a go of it. Start a family even. He chuckled at the thought of little ones climbing on his lap and playing around the cabin.

He noticed that all the birds that had been chirping so loudly and merrily in the pine trees as he swung along were gradually going silent. He looked up. One lone turkey buzzard was making big lazy circles in the bright sky. Something must have died, he thought, still thinking about Marie and the phantom *pirogue*.

Suddenly Frenchy Carrefours felt a *whoosh* near his head, as if the big bird in the sky had taken a pass at him. His lilting whistle ceased on a down note.

The silence was deafening.

★   ★   ★

The asphalt road was already sticky in the March sunlight, and the damp left from the rain the night before filled the air with a steamy heat.

Myron Duson was not in a good mood. The catnaps he had taken while riding had not rested him, and the demise of the Olds infuriated him.

Carrefours was a fool. Duson had known immediately that the Cajun had cut the oil line. Now he intended to cut

Frenchy loose and go on alone. But first, he had to take care of business.

The pines on either side of the road seemed to hold in the heat, rather than provide the comfort of shade, so he took off his jacket and folded it neatly over his arm. His hat was not wide-brimmed enough to keep the sun off his neck, but it helped keep the sun out of his eyes as he trudged onward, scanning the roadsides ahead for any hint of an opening in the woods.

Soon he spotted a break and what looked like a cow path of sorts leading back toward the other direction. Without hesitation, Duson jumped on to the faint trail and double-timed it, in spite of the heat, back towards where the car had broken down. He had no intention of letting Frenchy get away with his treachery. Besides, the Cajun knew too much. It violated all of Duson's principles to let him survive to tell the tale.

He kept pushing himself forward, sustained by his anger and desire for revenge. He knew the Cajun had a head start on him, but he probably wasn't expecting to be followed. Duson kept glancing up at the sky, trying to follow the movement of the sun. He could begin going in circles if he lost his bearings.

Finally, he spotted a tell-tale wavering in the brush ahead, then heard the whistled notes of Frenchy's tune. He flung down his jacket and began looking about for something he could use as a weapon. A sturdy branch with a knot on the end came to hand. Myron Duson hefted the cudgel and swung it about. Yes, it would do nicely.

Moving forward, more stealthily now, he realized that the man in front of him was oblivious to his surroundings. The Cajun was strolling along, whistling an old folk song, as if he hadn't a care in the world. A lot he knew!

Duson crept up behind Frenchy, as close as he could, raised his club high over his head, and brought it down with a dull thud against the other man's temple. Blood immediately spurted from the wound.

Again and again, Duson brought down the heavy stick, beating the Cajun to a pulp. At last, sated, he threw the stick to one side, checked the lifeless body for a pulse, then meticulously went through his belongings, removing anything of value and all identity.

So much for you, mon ami, Duson thought with satisfaction. *Laissez les bons temps rouler, indeed!*

★ ★ ★

Forty-five minutes later, back on the road, Duson spotted a break in the bushes along the fence line, with a muddy drive leading away from the asphalt. Rounding a curve, he could see big trees growing some distance from the road — and beneath their sheltering shade huddled a small tin-roofed frame house.

He almost grinned in glee, but he saved the energy for later. This was the break he needed, and he must make it work for him. Nobody must know that he was coming until he sized up the situation.

He turned aside and climbed through a tight barbed-wire fence, catching himself painfully several times on its barbs before he made it all the way through and emerged on the other side. An unkempt field of brush and weeds lay between him and the house, screening his approach if he stooped and took reasonable care. He was no woodsman by any means, but he had learned through necessity how to move across open land without being detected. In due time, he found himself at the back of a neat dooryard, where stalks of spring jonquils still stood up stiffly under japonica bushes. There was no sign of any living being about, though a rusty pickup sat in a shed of sorts, which was just a tin roof held up by four untrimmed posts, weathered to a satiny gray.

He ducked under a low sycamore limb and moved silently across a flowerbed toward the kitchen door, which was screened by a big overgrown dogwood, peppered with newly opened white blooms. As he came around the bush, an old woman popped out the back door and into the yard, holding a pan of scraps and calling, 'Here, kitty-kitty!' at the top of her voice.

She saw him before he could reach her side, and her mouth opened wide. He didn't wait to learn whether a greeting or a scream was about to come out of it. He hit her expertly on the side of her scrawny neck. When she went down, legs jerking reflexively like a beheaded chicken, he leaned over and methodically crushed her skull with a whitewashed rock he plucked from the edge of the path.

A gruff roar interrupted him, and he straightened to meet the assault of a man, presumably the woman's husband, who was charging him with a crutch held like a spear. A gray ruffle of thinning hair stood straight up on the old man's head, and his eyes were wild with rage and grief.

It was no great trick to take this new threat out as well. No witness had ever lived to testify against Myron Duson, he thought in satisfaction. No witness ever — except a single skinny woman back in east Texas.

Once he was certain the place was deserted, he went through the house at his leisure, searching for money, weapons or anything else that might be useful. He found a hoard of dimes in a fruit jar — too heavy for fast travel, not worth the taking, he decided. He located an ancient ten-gauge shotgun, but its load had corroded in the chamber. Worse than no good.

Then he found a copy of *Sports Afield* with a five-dollar bill marking a place in it. Leafing through to see if more bills might be inside, he ran across a familiar name staring up at him from a page devoted to dog enthusiasts.

'ALLISON FROST VERNIER, breeder extraordinary,' was the caption beneath a photo of an elderly woman standing in a dog run among a half-dozen English setters. An accompanying article was evidently about her breeding kennels and the success of her setters in field trials.

Frost! That was the name of the people in Templeton. A coincidence, perhaps, but Duson had not become the feared man he was through ignoring such hunches. He made note of the location of that farm. Might give him a handle on the gun dealer, he thought. You never knew when such knowledge might come in handy.

When he was done searching the house and had finished off a superb custard pie and a quart of milk from the refrigerator, he went out and searched the man's body for the pickup keys. He found nothing in the man's pockets; but to his amazement, the keys were stuck in the ignition, the door was unlocked, and the vehicle was gassed up and ready to roll.

What sort of place was this, he wondered, where people could go about leaving things of value so unsecured? But he didn't have time to worry about that. Instead, he put the old junker in gear and rolled away out the drive and onto the asphalt road in a cloud of smelly blue smoke.

Once he reached civilization, he would look for a decent car to steal. This one would last, he hoped, for as long as he needed it. But if it didn't, there were always other cars out there — and other car-owners to remove from the equation.

★   ★   ★

Washington Shipp was not resting easy in his mind. The Frosts, thank heavens, had gotten well away now, and were staying with their elderly relative over in Louisiana. Only Wash and Amy knew exactly where they were, and that should have reassured him.

But for some reason he kept returning to the identity of the gun thief who had looked so much like Martin Fewell. Wash had a gut feeling he wasn't through with that bastard, no matter that he had been stopped and almost apprehended across the Louisiana line. Two of his henchmen were now in custody. They weren't talking yet, but in time they would be convinced otherwise, he felt certain, knowing how the Louisiana police operated.

For that reason, he had asked Amy to keep a special file of any new bulletins issued out of Louisiana, particularly those concerning stolen cars, physical assaults, or burglaries of any kind. He hadn't realized how much paperwork that would entail, but he doggedly plowed through the morning's stack, looking for anything at all that might ring his internal alarm.

Beside him was a large map of the east Texas-western Louisiana area, and he had circled the point at which the van and two of its riders had been apprehended. Now he was plotting spots at which cars had been stolen, beginning with one that had disappeared only a few blocks from the place where Duson and his unknown henchman had disappeared.

It was amazing how many vehicles had been stolen in Louisiana in the past day and a half. He worked at it for more than an hour, blessedly uninterrupted by any local catastrophe worse than a stray cow in Mrs. Blasingame's vegetable garden. When he was finished, the map was fairly well-dotted with tiny red marks, but he could see that at least three of them lay in a direct line running south and east along Interstate 10.

That was a mind-boggler, for the pair might be heading toward New Orleans instead, where they could disappear easily and permanently into the depths of the metropolis. Still, his instinct said otherwise.

'They've turned west again,' he muttered to himself, staring at the map. 'I'd bet my life on it.'

Amy interrupted him with another bulletin. But this one had brought a flush of excitement to her round face.

'Here's one from right across the state line. An old couple was found yesterday afternoon near Merriville, Louisiana, beaten to death. Their house was ransacked and their pickup was stolen. A red Chevy, 1973 model, rusty, dent in right front fender. The license number is probably no good now, but here it is.' She thrust the papers into his hands and watched his face as he read.

Shipp felt a chill go down his spine. This was right. This was it. He had known the predator was coming back to make sure of his kill, and here was the clue he had been waiting for. The brutality of the crime convinced him that it must be Duson's work.

'Here's something else,' said Amy, handing him another bulletin. 'They found one of the stolen cars a couple of miles east of the murder site. The engine was frozen up, and the oil line had been perforated. The local sheriff thinks that only one man committed the murders. It rained the night before and only one set of tracks crossed the flowerbed at the back of the house. And there wasn't a mark on the mud in the driveway except the tracks where the pickup went out. So it doesn't look like the perp drove into the property — only out with the stolen pickup.'

He nodded. 'That means the other one's left the game. He was an expert mechanic, from what I can gather, so if that oil line was holed, he did it on purpose. Now, where's *he* going? Not here, or he'd have come on ahead with Duson. We may be able to scratch him off our list for now, but that doesn't do us much good. He wasn't the dangerous one.'

'Here's the rest of the report,' Amy said.

He looked through the papers she handed him. 'Fingerprints found on the hood latch of the abandoned car match those of one Myron Duson, most recently of Beaumont, Texas, a convicted felon now wanted in Texas for robbery and assault; and Étienne 'Frenchy' Carrefours, of Calcasieu Parish, Louisiana, a known car thief and associate of Maurice Boulangère, fence and dealer in stolen goods, New Orleans. He's had six arrests, but no convictions.' He looked up at Amy. 'These must be our boys,' he said, his tone deceptively soft. 'They're headed this way, at least Duson is. We'd better stake out the Frost house. He'll go there for sure.'

'Who can be spared?' she asked. 'Whit Lambert's been sick with the flu. Joseph went out to see about that stray cow in the garden, but when he gets back he's scheduled to take night duty tonight. Both our late-shift people are supposed to be in Austin tomorrow to testify in that DWI/vehicular homicide case.'

'Damn!' Why was it that when you most needed manpower, everyone was out of pocket? Wash chewed at his thumbnail, thinking hard. 'Amy, could you stay here tonight and use the cot in the office, just in case anything comes in that needs handling? I could stake out the Frost house myself. That would leave Joseph free to patrol, and he could come if I needed him. Okay?'

Amy might groan a bit, but he knew that in reality she loved to fill in like this when there was a need. She fancied herself as a policewoman, he knew, a role where she could forget her about age and arthritic knees.

'He's on his way,' he said, looking down at the map. 'From Merriville, he could have driven right here into the county before dark last night and be hidden out somewhere close by already. We'd better be on the watch for him. You call Joseph and tell him the drill.'

The day went by slowly after that, filled with paperwork. From time to time, Wash looked up at the clock and wondered where Myron Duson was, what he was planning, and how he could go about ambushing the bastard if he came to the Frost house that night. He didn't, of course, know Duson at all. That meant he would have to be extremely cautious.

But Washington Shipp knew how to be cautious.

If he got himself into bad trouble, his wife Jewel would kill him for sure.

6

Martin Fewell had been driving for hours, it seemed to him. His neck was stiff, and his back was cramped, and he needed to pee something awful.

The urge that was propelling him westward, along the irregular jogs and windings of Highway 190, was still strong enough to keep him from stopping too often, and he wanted to put such pauses off until he was forced to get gasoline. Only after he had crossed the state line into Texas without incident did he feel sufficiently at ease to pull over into a logging track beside the highway to relieve himself.

He couldn't help but notice a shabby pickup truck pulled up in the same spot, out of sight of the road behind him. Somebody hunting, he figured; though whatever it was, it was probably illegal this early in the spring.

He looked about, but nobody was in

sight. Then he got out and stretched the cramps out of his joints. A short trip behind a clump of young pine trees got rid of another problem, and he went back to get into his pickup, which, while it was no Porsche, was still better than the old wreck blocking the road.

Some old instinct made him stop.

Suddenly on the alert, Martin spun on his heel, ducking at the same time, and let his reflexes take over. His fist thudded into a hard belly while he still felt the breeze of the blow that had just missed his head. Then he was on the ground, trying desperately with what strength he had left to hold down his assailant.

The man beneath him was as big as he was, but harder and younger. Surely he would be no match for the nasty tricks Martin had spent a lifetime learning, in and out of prison.

Yet he was.

Martin fought him all the way, tripping him, eye-gouging, trying for a knee in the groin; but the fellow knew how to counter all his moves. This was an ex-con, without any doubt.

At last the attacker jerked free of Martin and hurled himself into the pickup, in which Fewell had left the keys. With a roar, the truck started; and before the older man could reach it, the driver slammed it into reverse and disappeared in a cloud of mud spatters.

Fewell stood in the quiet of the pine woods, his anger growing by the minute. That bastard hadn't given him a chance, just swung and hoped to kill. He'd met too many of that sort in his criminal career to mistake the intention. And now the attacker was off and gone in the only thing Fewell owned in all the world, outside of his few clothes, which were in his old suitcase in the camper.

The roar of the engine disappeared westward up 190. Well, by god, he wasn't one to stand around and let someone take off with his property.

He turned to the stranded truck and looked inside. Well-kept seats, but old. The body was rusty and dented. He opened the hood and peered into the engine. It smelled hot, but he didn't think it had seized up. Probably the thing was slow and rattly, and when it got hot, its driver had just decided to take the next best thing that came along.

It was Martin's own fault for turning off the highway when he did. If he had just gone on to the next station, that bastard would have snared somebody else with some hard-luck story out on the main road. Probably leaving the owner dead in a ditch, if his style held true.

He checked the gauges. There wasn't much gas left, and the oil pressure wavered around once he got the engine started, but it settled down at last. It needed water, and he knew he'd have to fill the radiator soon, but he thought he could nurse it along. There was a Mom-and-Pop grocery and station just a few miles up the road, if he remembered correctly.

He decided to chance it. That character might have thought he'd left Martin Fewell stranded out here in the woods, but he didn't know who he was dealing with. And he'd follow the snake clear across Texas if he had to, just to get his own back. The little money left in his pocket would buy gas and oil, and if he had to do without food for a while, well he'd done that before.

Still cursing under his breath, he crept backward out of the logging track, looked both ways carefully, and backed onto the highway. Nobody was in sight. He pulled off in low, feeling out each gear as he shifted, making sure there was nothing badly wrong with the vehicle he now drove.

By the time he reached the store, the radiator was boiling again, but a fill of water and five dollars' worth of gas seemed to settle the truck down pretty well. He got an extra can of oil, just in case the thing burned a lot. Then he set off in pursuit of the hijacker.

That sapsucker might think he was tough, but Martin Fewell had invented tough, and he intended to use every bit of it when he found his nemesis.

★   ★   ★

Was he was losing his touch? Even as he pulled away from the scene of his latest

123

disaster, Myron continued fretting over it.

Out of his last four encounters, two of the victims had survived! That was a bad average — the sort that could get a man sent up to Huntsville for that lethal injection they kept claiming was so humane.

He had no intention of getting caught and even less of dying. But that old guy back there in the woods had been a tough son-of-a-bitch. Learned his stuff in a place with barred windows, he'd bet his life on that. And there was something familiar about him, too. He'd have to think on that — try to remember if and when they had crossed paths before.

Just getting away from the man uninjured had been a pretty hard thing to do. Killing him would have been something that Myron wasn't quite certain he could have accomplished. Not without more time and hassle than he was willing to risk.

The truck he now drove was, however, many cuts above the clunker he had stolen after killing the old couple. It had been cared for, that was clear. As he rattled along the newly widened highway toward Jasper, he kept a cautious eye on the oil gauge. Frenchy had taught him that much at least. But he needn't have worried. It sat steady, while the gas gauge was what he found he must watch most closely. That truck guzzled gasoline as if it were air.

And he hadn't all that much cash money with him. He'd relied heavily on being paid a hefty sum for the gun collection, and the stash he'd picked up in Alexandria hadn't been a lot. That damned Bollivar!

But he shook away the thought. Done was done, and there was no point in worrying about it, for Bollivar was no threat to him.

No, the woman witness: she was the big threat. And that old man back there who was still alive to yell assault and robbery when he made it to a town. Myron had never left so many loose ends before, and he was mightily rattled at the thought that his magic touch was failing him.

He slowly passed by a highway patrol car, but the driver paid no heed to him.

So there hadn't been a complaint filed on this pickup yet. Maybe he'd hurt that old buzzard enough so that he would lie there in the woods and die.

But that was wishful thinking, and he knew it. The older man had come nearer injuring him than the other way around. That sucker had taken his lumps in a prison yard, or Myron was no expert. He was still trying to remember where he might have seem him. Never mind. It would come to him in time.

He finally reached Jasper and filled up at a big Exxon station on the corner where two main highways crossed. So far, he had watched his speed and had stopped at every sign without sliding through. He sure as hell didn't want any hick lawman impeding him in his business.

When he pulled out again, heading northwest to avoid Toledo Bend Lake, he was a model of propriety. But when he turned on State Highway 63, he sped up just a bit. He wanted to get into Templeton just after dark.

First he'd find a place to stay where he

could keep completely out of sight. When it was really late and the burg had rolled up its sidewalks, he would go out to that big old house and finish the job Crowley had started. With any luck, there'd be time enough to search the place again for anything they might have missed the first time around.

He stopped at a café and ate before dark. He idled over coffee, watching traffic whiz past on the road, waiting until it was that lazy hour when everyone was at supper and the police'd had a long day but hadn't been relieved for the evening.

When he was satisfied that everything was to his liking, he paid his tab and got back into the pickup. Maybe it had worked out best to drive a working man's truck, looking sober and respectable. If he'd lifted something like a Lincoln, which he'd planned to do, that would have been too flashy and noticeable.

There was a fleabag motel just outside the Templeton city limits. He checked in using the name he found on the registration in the pocket of the truck: Martin Fewell. Sounded stolid and dull.

Probably that tough back in the pine woods had stolen the truck himself, for he hadn't acted like a normal citizen who always froze and let you slaughter them like sheep.

He was tired. He didn't like to drive, and he heartily cursed Carrefours for letting that comfortable Olds go sour on them. But the traitor had already paid the price for crossing Myron Duson, and there wasn't much point in wasting energy on a dead man.

He lay on top of the faded chenille bedspread, still wearing his shoes, and turned on the TV. There was a news item about the murder in Louisiana, and to his horror he heard his name being mentioned.

Fingerprints? He'd wiped everything carefully, always did. Compulsively! How had they tied him to that crime so quickly? They also mentioned Frenchy, but that was little comfort. Where had he left his prints? On the Olds? He had wiped the door handle, the dash, the seat cover, the outside of the doorframe. He always did that.

And then he thought of it. When he touched the hood. Someplace there, he had left a print he didn't realize was on it. A hidden place . . . the latch under the hood? That had to be it!

He was going soft. His skill was slipping, and his knack was dulling with age and overuse. He had to get back on track, or he would be a goner.

He shut off the tube and turned on his side. He must sleep now. His interior timer would wake him when the night was at the correct point in its progress. He knew he could rely on that, if nothing else.

Tonight would see him back on track. Tonight would turn his career around, for good and all. With that thought, he dozed off, secure in his control of the future.

★   ★   ★

Wash yawned, but he didn't move a muscle. His youth spent hunting in the riverbottoms had trained him well for stalking men. The shelter of the Chinese holly was thick, the glossy leaves forming a prickly barrier between him and the light that Frost had left burning in the utility room off the back porch.

He didn't allow a rustle or a shiver of branches to betray his presence. There had been no sign of anyone in the grounds, but that didn't mean Duson might not be within arm's reach of him. Wash had learned that in an even harsher school than prison. The forests along the Nichayac could be crawling with gators, water moccasins, or even cougars, and you never would know until it was too late. But far worse than those natural predators were the illegal hunters that roamed the bottoms. They would kill you without a second thought or a backwards glance.

He let out his breath as silently as possible and tried to keep a constant sweeping watch on the open space around the back door of the Frost home. There was a sudden feeling of tension in the air. Wash realized that the mockingbird who had been going through all his loud and glorious repertory in the tall sycamore standing sentry beside the back porch was quiet now. He tried to gauge in his mind just how long it had been since the birdsong had ceased.

Now, even the first timid peepers of spring stilled their shrill piping voices — and there was only the faint whisper of a light breeze sighing through the sharp-angled leaves of his sheltering holly.

Wash had developed an instinct back there in his youth that had saved his life more than once. He knew, somehow, and with some innate sense that wasn't quite physical, when a poisonous snake or some other dangerous critter was sharing his hiding place. And not even his elders had been aware of their presence. In fact, he'd felt such impending dangers many times over his lifetime, even though no sight or sound betrayed them.

Now he knew, without a shadow of a doubt, there was someone on the other side of the holly bush. Someone else's ears also strained at the night, trying to detect anything that didn't fit into the picture. And someone else's breath was being controlled with great care, even as Wash was managing his own so as not to betray his presence. He felt the stress in those other invisible muscles. He understood on a primitive level the wariness and the caution of that other one — who even now thought he was stalking his prey.

With thoughts of Lily and Stony Frost, in their far away refuge by now, and of his own precious wife, safely at home with the boy, Wash slowly eased the bulk of his weight onto his left foot. The dried holly leaves, which had accumulated for years beneath the huge twists of branches, made no sound at all, for he brought his weight to bear steadily, thus eliminating all possibility of crunching. The nearby branches swept harmlessly past his shoulders with no telltale scrape of leaf against the cloth.

As carefully as if he were about to face a cougar in the depths of the forest, Wash moved out of his nook and around the large bush. He expected at any moment to see the dark shape of his adversary.

There was a sudden blink of the dim light shining out from the porch. A solid body had passed across its faint beam.

Alarmed, he strained forward, his forty-five in hand — but the watcher was gone, vanished like a ghost into the thick growth tangling the acreage around the house.

Taking out his flashlight, the lawman examined the ground about the holly bush. Here was a scuffed spot, as if a big foot had rested in the same place for some time. There was a skid mark where the quarry had taken off like a scalded cat.

Wash sank back on his heels and stared thoughtfully into the multiple shadows of the trees. This was a man with the instincts of a cat. He knew, just as Wash knew, when there was an enemy at hand. They had waited, like two rivals, on either side of the stickery complex of holly, seeking to discover whatever it was that had set off their inner warnings. And, almost at the same instant in time, they had decided to move.

Wash Shipp shivered inside his skin. He didn't like this feeling — as if he were somehow akin to that dangerous creature of the night shaped like a man. But he also knew, deep down inside, that he now understood Myron Duson far better than he had ever thought he might. And that gave him an advantage.

Sighing, he went to the back door and used the key Stony had left with him. He had to see if Duson had been inside, rooting around to see what he could find. Although now he wondered if he had not interrupted the man before he could manage an entry.

Still, being thorough was Wash's main attribute, and he went into the service porch and on through into the kitchen. There he saw at once that his quarry had already been in the house. The Frost kitchen was always both tidy and spotless. Now it showed signs of having been searched hastily. Drawers were pulled out, the silverware had been disarranged, and the papers on the small work table had been shuffled about and left scattered. Wash hoped fervently that neither of the Frosts had left any clues concerning their intended destination.

But Stony was no fool. Wash was pretty confident that he would have been careful. There was no point in going into the rest of the house. The man had been here. Now he was gone.

He needed to let Stony and Lily know as soon as he got back to the office. That might seem like a paranoid move to some, but when it came to Myron Duson, Washington Shipp felt no amount of precaution was foolish.

The man was every bit as dangerous as any of the wild predators he had encountered in his youth. And, even more unsettling, he was just as unpredictable.

★   ★   ★

His heart pounding, Duson rolled his waiting pickup out of the side road in which he had left it and switched on the engine. He had not thought he'd come back to it so quickly — and without accomplishing his goal.

Getting into the house had been easy enough. It was so big and rambling, though, that searching it thoroughly was simply not feasible. It was clear that the inhabitants were no longer living in the house, for he had checked the bedrooms upstairs first, and they were empty and bereft of clothing. The little desk in the kitchen had obviously been the center of business for the household, but among all the papers and ledgers he found there, he discovered no indication of any intention to leave their home or where they might have gone.

Damn that woman! She seemed to lead a charmed life all right. He'd have to break that spell!

And why was someone out here at night watching the house, when he, her attacker, had been reported over in Louisiana, running away from the scene of the crime as fast as he could? Duson was disgusted with the situation, but even more so with himself. He was not used to losing his cool and breaking his cover as he had back there in the semi-darkness. And the other man watching the house had known Myron Duson was there. He was sure of it! Yet Duson had not sensed until it was almost too late that there had been anyone else on the grounds at all.

That, of course, meant the fellow

shared the same abilities Myron had used so successfully over the years. He always knew when an enemy was near. He heard when there was no sound. He felt the presence of another through his pores and read the intentions of that being unerringly. So if this man, police or deputy or whatever else he might be, had all that in common with Duson, he might also know even more.

For instance, he had known, apparently, that his quarry would come back to the scene of the crime to finish the job left undone. And he *had* known — Duson was convinced of it. Not only that, but tonight's risky maneuver had been an exercise in futility, because the woman was not there at all. She and the gun-dealer had been moved out of harm's way.

He felt a jolt inside as a hazy memory returned. That magazine in the old people's house! It contained a story about a woman with the same name. Was she, perhaps, a relative? Was it too coincidental?

All his instincts said, 'Yes, she *must* be

a relative!' Duson had memorized the name and the town simply because it was his habit to be thorough, to leave nothing undone or to chance.

His spirits picked up and he chuckled as the pickup bounced along a dirt track. A few miles along, it intersected a farm-to-market road that would take him back to the highway. In time, and with some study of his local maps, the route most certainly would lead him to the farm of Allison Frost Vernier.

An old woman and the crippled gun dealer could never hope to protect the witness from him. The thought of finishing his task filled him with warmth, and he drove along humming, tapping his fingers on the steering wheel in a rhythmic accompaniment to his untuneful voice.

★   ★   ★

Allison Vernier had not fully realized how much she'd missed having her family about her. After Louis, her husband, died, she had flung herself into her work with total commitment so as to avoid self-pity and loneliness, and that had worked very well.

Still, there was nothing like having your own kin about you to help the time pass — even if they sometimes were irritating. Lily, for instance, was not what Allison liked to think of as a true example of the Frost family resilience. In Allison's opinion, an attack by a burglar shouldn't have had such a dramatic effect on her. That timidity and shrinking from strangers must be, her great-aunt thought, a direct result of Lily's brief but devastating flirtation with the drug culture. Allison had read about all the ill effects that resulted from the misuse of drugs. Drugs were dangerous, she concluded, and she was convinced that a government could rule its citizens like robots by promoting drug abuse among them. Very soon they would be too weak and afraid to resist, and the mere possibility of such a plot, no matter how far-fetched, made her furious.

To think of her own niece being so passive and fear-driven made her even angrier. She was determined at all costs to bring Lily out of her present frame of mind — even if it required major shock therapy. Allison knew herself to have the capacity for that — Louis had often told her it was kind of God to make her so caring for people and animals, for otherwise she would have been too dangerous to have around. He meant it as a joke, of course. Still, there was a kind of truth to it.

She mopped her forehead with the back of one wrist, pushing back the crisp white curls that insisted on straggling from beneath the net under which she confined them.

Her dogs milled about her feet, licking her elbows, knees and hands indiscriminately. All that brought the first smile of the day to her face; if nothing else, she was a fool for her setters.

Lily and Stony were bringing in fresh hay for bedding for the dogs behind the smaller of the two tractors. Allison was glad to see Stony looked much healthier than he had when they first arrived. He'd been pale and drawn the night before. But today his eyes were bright, and if his cheeks were not rosy, it was because his olive complexion didn't allow it.

'Where you want this load?' he called cheerfully.

'Take it right into the middle run and put it into the boxes there. That's where the pregnant bitches have their litters. Then let's go on up to the house and cool off a bit. For spring, it's getting mighty hot.'

She finished feeding the group in her pen, checked to see that the others in the line of dog runs had eaten well, then gratefully led the others toward her big comfortable house where Maggie had iced tea and sandwiches ready for them.

Allison always ate an early light lunch after her labors in the kennels, for she began her day well before dawn. Stony and his sister, without Allison requesting them or even hinting at it, had adapted their own schedules to hers — and willingly joined her every morning, helping her with the chores. That allowed Cephus, who would otherwise have been doing such work, to mend fences or mow pastures or tend the few choice head of

Angus cattle that were a part of the Vernier spread. It was a wonderful arrangement, Allison thought.

Having people who understood and appreciated music and art, and with whom one could talk politics and international affairs, was even better. Her mealtimes had become stimulating get-togethers instead of mere pauses in the day to fuel her body. Allison had decided, without daring as yet to mention it to her kin, that she wanted them to visit her more often — even after the current emergency had ended. She worried that it might seem selfish to ask them to spend more time with one who was, after all, the contemporary of their grandfather. Today, however, she decided to risk it.

The lunch table was set with her favorite green Depression glass dishes and goblets, confirming that Maggie had decided it was now summer, whether or not the calendar officially declared it so. Allison plopped into her chair and grinned at Stony, who had turned up his glass of iced tea and drained it.

'You know, Aunt Allie, it's wonderful to

be outside doing things. I never knew how much I was missing it. My folks always seemed to think that because my body was twisted, I couldn't do anything physical at all.'

Lily nodded.

'And I was a *girl*, so they didn't want me to do anything but girlie things. I like active work a lot better. And Martin . . . ' She paused, as if astonished that she actually had mentioned his name. 'Martin just dived in and did things,' she went on. 'And he never minded if I went right along with him. But he thought I ought to be just as enthusiastic about hurting people as I was about loading logs or running a cotton picker.'

Ah! Lily had opened up a bit. This was a good sign, Allison thought.

She poured more tea all around and said, 'Your mother was raised to be a lady. Dratted nuisance, of course, and she deserved better. She had the makings of a real person under all those layers of foolishness.' She passed the platter of sandwiches, noting the glance that Lily turned toward her brother. 'It's not easy getting over a misguided childhood, but let me tell you it's worth it,' Allison continued after a moment. 'My own mother thought she was going to make a lady out of me. But I was a Frost, and my grandmother was still alive to show me what a person *ought* to be. She'd tackle a bear and give it the first two bites.'

Lily giggled, choked on a bite, and was thumped soundly on the back by Stony. The sound of their laughter filled Allison with a feeling of great well-being.

Maggie came soundlessly into the room and bent to whisper into her ear. The feeling of satisfaction popped like a bubble. Allison rose, excused herself, and followed Maggie out of the room to the telephone.

'Miz Vernier?' she heard when she picked up. 'This is Sheriff Washington Shipp, back here in Nichayac County. I'm sorry to tell you, this, but Myron Duson was in Stony's house last night. That doesn't mean he found anything to guide him to you, but it won't hurt to be on guard, do you think?'

'Thank you, Sheriff,' Allison said, her

heart thudding icily in her chest. 'We'll keep an eye open and take all precautions. Please let us know if you learn anything more, will you?'

She returned to the table and took her place, and she knew her expression had revealed to Stony and Lily that trouble was in the wind.

7

Shipp made it back to his office in jig time. Amy was asleep on the cot in the back room, her cheeks rosy, her white hair rumpled. He shook her regretfully. She was old now, and needed her rest, but this was important.

'Get a hold of that sheriff over in Bossier Parish, will you, Amy, just as soon as he's in his office? I need to make a run over there and check out that murder site. I'm missing something, I know, and I need to stand in that bastard's tracks and smell him out.'

'What time is it?' She yawned, reaching up to push several huge hairpins back into the braided snails of hair that covered each of her ears.

'Four-oh-five,' he said.

The pot was plugged in as usual, and he poured hot water into a Styrofoam cup and spooned in instant coffee. He was chilled to the bone, though the

146

spring night was more damp than cold. Learning that his quarry had the same finely honed instincts he possessed was a worrying thing, and he thought that might have shaken him more than he knew.

Amy reached for the battered alarm clock sitting on the spindly chair beside the cot. 'I'm setting this for six, Wash. You go on home and get a little sleep, if you can, and as soon as I get word I'll call you,' she told him. 'If I were your wife, I'd throw you out, Wash. I don't know how Jewel stands it. You're not at home any more than a tomcat.'

He grinned at her, finishing his coffee. 'But for very different reasons, Amy. For very different reasons.'

He switched off the overhead light and left her to what remained of the night, but he didn't go home. Instead, he drove again to the Frost house, hidden behind its screen of hollies and crepe myrtles, crouching beneath its overgrown oaks and pines.

Using his flashlight, Wash first moved around the south side of the silent

147

building, examining the ground carefully for tracks. It looked like Duson had come to the property from the front and gone straight to the kitchen door. Bold bastard! He must have hidden his car down the road, where a track led off into the woods, and walked back in the cover of the roadside undergrowth.

Then Wash continued around the house on the north side, keeping close to the thick clumps of bridal wreath and camellias until he found more tell-tale tracks. Duson had emerged from the house not far from the holly under which Shipp had hidden. He'd stood there for some time, still as a rock. The edges of his tracks weren't blurred with movement, but the prints themselves were well sunk into the damp soil, showing that he had remained there for a while.

Just as he had himself, Wash thought. Like two jungle animals, each sensing the presence of the other, they had hidden there listening, feeling outward with every perception they had, trying to get the jump when the time came on the enemy who was perceived but not seen. He shivered hard, feeling again that raw moment of awareness.

The man had run north, pushing through the privet hedge and moving into the mixed hardwood and pine forest that formed the northern two acres of the Frost estate. The interloper had reconnoitered the place well, Shipp figured, before the first break-in. Now he knew the best approach and the best retreat from this dark house.

It was becoming lighter in the east, the first pale streak lying along the horizon, where it could be seen between the big trees. There was dew thick on Shipp's windshield, and he turned on the wipers for a moment before backing out of the driveway and swiveling to avoid the huge landmark tree at its entrance.

Then he stopped, staring back at the face of the house, just becoming visible in the light of dawn. It looked enigmatic and smug, like a cat that had caught its prey in the night. He could almost envision the tail of a mouse hanging out of the rounded lips of the upper and lower porches.

Wash shook his head sharply to remove the illusion. That was nonsense and he knew it. The problem had come from outside that gloomy structure, not from within. And no matter how dark and overburdened with heavy antique furniture, no Victorian house could spook Washington Shipp.

He wasn't entirely sure he could say the same about Myron Duson.

★   ★   ★

Myron Duson pulled into an economy motel just before daylight and parked behind the office, so his battered pickup was invisible from the highway. He didn't think that lawman back there in Templeton had seen him — or his vehicle either — but he wasn't about to take any chances on that possibility.

Driving by day was not a smart move. He was tired and jumpy, and it had been hours since he had gotten a good rest. He decided to sleep the daylight away here, grab a good meal, then set off again on his quest come twilight.

The wide spot in the road where he had stopped was so small it didn't really qualify as a town at all. There was a big truck stop with attached café and garage, a grocery across the state highway, and the motel a mile down the road where the state road crossed a U.S. highway heading north and south. Trees surrounded the double line of cottages, coming right up to the doors. That gave concealment as he came and went, which was always good.

He registered with a sleepy clerk who probably could hardly recall his own name even when he was wide awake, and got himself under cover before early risers began driving to work. Tomorrow he would steal another vehicle and head for northern Louisiana and that big farm where the old woman named Frost lived.

If his quarry wasn't there . . . but he knew in his gut that the crippled gun dealer *was* there. And that tall lanky woman who had escaped his vengeance . . . yes, she would be there, too.

★   ★   ★

Washington Shipp turned off toward Merriville and made a series of sharp-angled turns that took him past the local schoolhouse and onto the farm road heading toward Ragley. The deputy who had met him near the river bridge was driving faster than seemed reasonable on the narrow road, and Wash stomped down on the gas to keep him in sight. They turned sharply right and left after going through Ragley, a town even smaller than Merriville, and crossed the railroad. Beyond that the deputy slowed somewhat, and in a few more miles he braked to turn into a steep drive leading between overhanging bushes. It was still muddy, churned up by the passage of many vehicles.

His wheels spun a bit, but Wash gunned the Chevy up the slope and turned aside to park on the grass beside the deputy's car. Once he stood in front of the neat little house, he felt a sudden stab of both anger and regret. Proud people had lived here, making work substitute for money. The ship-lap siding was freshly whitewashed, the tin roof shining with aluminum paint. Everything was clean, neat, and orderly.

Though the front porch sagged beneath the weight of years, it was obviously freshly swept, where muddy shoes had tracked their prints between steps and door. Pots of ferns sat along the sides of the porch, and vines climbed from other pots that hung from hooks screwed into the beams of the roof.

It was too much like his own mother's house for comfort, Wash decided. He could almost see the tidy old lady who had last swept the porch and watered the plants as he climbed the steps and opened the screen door.

Inside it was cool and dark, in contrast to the bright daylight, and he paused, letting his eyes adjust. Then the feeling of familiarity came flowing back. The Greek Revival furniture told him that at some point these people had been better off. Books and magazines lay in straight-edged stacks on the floor beside the two rocking chairs, and more magazines were arranged on a library table along one wall.

'Nothing here to show what happened,' said the deputy. 'The old folks was found out back, the woman killed with a rock, the man beaten and strangled. I think the killer must've come through the house, because there's an empty pie pan on the kitchen table and an empty milk jug by the refrigerator, but I can't see any sign he come in here. Sheriff Elkin couldn't, either.'

Shipp nodded, but that old instinct was alert, on the job, telling him that Duson had stood here, almost in this very same spot. He had looked around — several scattered magazines on the table should have been piled neatly like the books on the floor.

He moved to examine them. A copy of *Sports Afield* was lying on its crumpled back cover, and as he straightened it, almost hearing his mother's familiar admonitions to be neat, it fell open at a photograph.

Allison Frost Vernier. He jerked alert, gripping the magazine.

The deputy looked at him questioningly, and Shipp asked, 'Do you mind if I take this? I've got an ongoing case that this might work into. Or does Sheriff Elkin want everything kept just as it is?'

'I'll ask. You want to come out back with me? I think he's out there again.'

They went down a narrow hall whose walls were tacked full of photographs of grandchildren and family gatherings, through the kitchen, and down the back steps. A worn mop hung from a hook in the door facing, just as his mother's always had. Again he felt a surge of intense sadness. Why should decent people die at the hands of a mad dog like Duson?

Elkins was pacing off the distance from the edge of the yard, stalking toward a scuffed spot in the spring grass. He looked up and said, 'You must be Sheriff Shipp from Templeton. Your dispatcher called to say you were comin'. You got something that ties into this?'

Shipp nodded. 'We had a burglary and attempted murder of a woman over our way a couple of days ago. Got a description that matches up with the prints you found on the abandoned car up the road. I think Myron Duson is the man we both want. And this magazine I found in the front room has an article about a woman that's kin to the victim of our crime. You mind if I take it? That's where the girl's gone, and if Duson saw this while he was here, it means he might go there to look for her.'

'Lord, man, take it! No magazine's going to help us catch that bastard. If you get him first, we want him. Better to hang a Murder One charge on him than anything less that he might get off on.'

Elkin wiped his pink forehead on his sleeve and stared back at the fence and its betraying loose strand of barbed wire. 'That's how he come in. Left the road up a ways, come through the pasture, kicked loose the wire, and come up on the old folks from the back. The old lady was lyin' right there, and next to her was a rock with her blood and brains on it.'

'Deputy Fuller says the old man was strangled,' Wash said. 'He must have heard something and come to see, you think?'

'You can see how his crutch is lyin' — I

think he come *at* the killer tryin' to get him with the only weapon he had, but it's hard to say for sure. However it was, we want this bastard the worst way. Good luck with findin' him, Sheriff. Keep us posted.' Elkins turned as another deputy came around the house and signaled for his attention.

Wash glanced at the scuffed spot, stained with dried blood, and shivered. Sometimes he was just as glad his own folks were safely dead and out of this crazy world. They'd lived good lives, and a car accident wasn't the worst way to go, by any means. At least it had been quick and relatively painless.

'Thanks,' Shipp called to Sheriff Elkins. 'I think I've got what I need.'

Then he hurried back to his car, turned around and headed toward Texas. He had no authority in Louisiana, but once he made some calls from his office in Templeton, he thought he might get some people in Bossier Parish on the ball.

He couldn't afford to take the chance that Myron Duson hadn't found that betraying name in the magazine left so carelessly sprawled across the table in that pitiful house. It was all but certain, at least to him, that the folks who lived there would never in a million years have left one of their publications out of order, much less crumpled up as it had been.

He sped along the blacktop road toward Merriville, his mind busy. What could he do to safeguard Stony and Lily and their elderly great-aunt? That was the problem that plagued him most as he headed for home.

★   ★   ★

The ancient clunker rattled and clanked, leaving a trail of blue exhaust as it moved. But at least it moved, and that was all Martin had expected of it. More than he had expected, in fact. It wouldn't have surprised him if the pickup had died on him before he passed Jasper. But it coughed and wheezed its slow way on into Templeton and let out its last gasp in front of the local junkyard — which, Fewell thought, provided a nice touch of irony.

The proprietor of the junkyard didn't bother to ask for proof of ownership, though if Martin recalled his Texas law correctly he probably should have. He paid fifty bucks for the steaming pile of junk, and Martin counted himself fortunate to get that much. It might be a tad illegal, but that bastard who'd taken his own truck was still on the move, and he had to have some traveling money. What was in his pocket was, as always, pretty skimpy.

Templeton hadn't changed much in the years since he'd shaken the dust off his feet and lured Lily Frost away from her protesting family. He wasn't surprised. In Fewell's experience, little towns like this one never built up enough industry to bring in the money needed to make much in the way of changes.

He struck out on foot, carefully avoiding the side street leading past the combined police station and jail. He crossed the intersecting highway that went north and south, and found the country road that led to the Frost place. His feet knew the way, although he had always driven it in his psychedelically painted van back in the old days.

It was a damn long walk, and it was getting close to dark before he spotted the big tree sticking out into the road that marked the Frost drive. He'd always wondered why they didn't cut the damned thing down. And all of Lily's convoluted explanations never convinced him that any tree, however old and historical, was worth a minute of the time it took to care for it, or an extra iota of inconvenience. Now, though, he was grateful for its nine-foot-thick trunk. The bushes around it had grown a lot in the intervening years, and he might have missed the drive altogether if it hadn't been for the oversized tree.

He checked the road, front and back, before darting across into the concealment of the crepe myrtles. The last sunset light did nothing to make his way easier, as he crept along the front porch, heading for the rear of the house. He'd never been allowed in the front door, a source of some bitterness to him at the time, so it seemed best to go in the way he knew. If

Lily and her crip of a brother were in there, he wanted to make sure they were all right. He wasn't quite certain yet of his motives, but he thought it best not to let them know he was there checking up on them. He had a funny feeling about what he was doing here, anyway. Not once in his life had he ever done anything just to help someone. It felt strange and unfamiliar, a little like putting on a new pair of shoes that didn't fit quite right.

Once he got to the back of the house, however, he realized that it was too quiet. No light shone through any window, though there was a dim glow emanating from the storeroom. The kitchen sat dark and silent behind the low overhang of the back porch.

Stony and Lily were gone from the house, and that was both obvious and good thinking on their part. But somehow he sensed that the possibility of danger hadn't been averted altogether. There was still a chill in his backbone that told him someone might be lurking about.

It was now getting very dark. The idea of walking all the way back to town and spending some of his scanty cash on a room wasn't all that inviting. Besides, he had this quirky feeling that something of import might well happen here before the night was over. This was a big empty house, all locked up, and Martin Fewell had learned to pick locks in his youth.

Before the last light left the sky, he was inside the place. It smelled old and a bit mildewy, but it wasn't the familiar kind of noxious odor Martin was accustomed to in his normal digs. This aroma was a richer, mellower sort of scent, compounded of leather and furniture polish, candles, and the acrid smell of cold fireplaces. The kitchen had its own essence, recognizable the instant he stuck his head in at the door. Generations of food seemed to linger in the air, along with the crisp lemony fragrance of dish detergent and cleanser.

He didn't dare turn on a light — who knew what sorts of neighbors might be able to see it and call the cops? — but his skilled, silent fingers checked out a cupboard that held crackers and canned meat. Another swift search found a can opener, and he ate his sparse meal standing at the sink.

Uncharacteristically, he rinsed out the can and swilled out the sink before turning to go over the rest of the house. No point in leaving random clues about. Martin had an uncomfortable feeling about Lily possibly discovering he had been there, prying into her private space and leaving a mess behind. He had treated her too badly in the past to expect much in the way of forgiveness; he didn't think he could bear to face her anger at his intrusion now.

He crept through the still rooms, still smelling the scent of wax and polish and old books. Something drew him to an upstairs window at last, to look down on the dark lawn. The blackness inside the house made the outside almost visible, the grass gray, the clumps of shrubbery encompassing dense shadows.

As Martin Fewell looked down from his perch, one blot of darkness moved away from another much larger one. A man was creeping over the grass. He merged into the shadow of the crepe myrtles along the walk; but before Martin could decide what to make of that puzzling sight, the other dark figure crept away just as stealthily from the same shelter.

Two men had been watching the house — possibly unaware of each other!

One must be the man who had tried to kill Lily, but who had the other one been? The law? Perhaps, but Fewell had no intention of hanging around to find out for sure.

He watched, silently, until the second shadow was well out of sight. Then he waited until the clock with the loud tick, which had been noting the half-hour with a light chime, cleared its throat and bonged once. Time to get to work.

There would be no sleep for him tonight, for he knew he must search this house thoroughly looking for some indication of Lily's whereabouts. He had to presume that her stalker had gone through everything before him, and he hoped no careless clue had been left to tell where the family had gone.

Whether she and her brother knew it or

not, they needed someone to keep watch over them, and Martin Fewell knew this was his calling. He'd earned his right for redemption the hard way, just as suffering had earned him a belated conscience. Hurting Lily had been the thing he did best. Now he was determined to make certain that nobody else took up that task.

*　*　*

Shipp pulled back into town by mid-afternoon and headed straight for the office to see if anything had come in that needed his immediate attention.

It was supposed to be the family's night out. On a regular basis he took Jewel and the boy either to visit Jewel's parents in the next county or out to dinner and a movie, or to any other pleasant activity their small town offered from time to time. It was the very least he could do to make up for all the times he couldn't be with them.

But Amy had a pile of paperwork waiting on his desk, and he began going through it carefully, signing letters, checking out reports, and making note of anything unusual.

Well before he was through, Amy tapped at his door. 'You've got a call from Ned Tubbs out at the junkyard. He got in a dead pickup this afternoon, and the fellow seemed to be in a terrible hurry. Ned fudged on the ownership papers, as the thing was good for nothing but scrap metal, but now he wants to talk to you about it.'

Wash could tell that she was afire with curiosity, for Ned Tubbs avoided the law as if he were a hardened criminal. Yet, in all the years he'd owned the junkyard, Shipp had never caught him doing anything illegal. 'I'll take it,' he said. 'Close the door, Amy.'

With a sniff, she went out, the door snapping shut behind her with an irritable click.

Shipp lifted the phone and said, 'Ned? What you got on your mind, man?'

There was a short silence. Then Ned coughed and snorted, as usual, before speaking. 'I had the radio on but I wasn't listenin' close. Then I caught a story about an old couple over Louisiana way — Bossier Parish — that got killed and their pickup was stole. Well, yesterday afternoon I took in a junker with Louisiana tags. I went out and looked, and sure enough, they match up with the ones the feller on the radio said. At least I think they do. You better come out and take a look at it, Sheriff.'

Better mark that on the calendar as a red-letter day, Shipp thought. The day Ned Tubbs actually invited the sheriff out to his place.

'Be right out, Ned,' he said. 'Don't you touch the thing any more than you can help, you hear? If it's the one we're lookin' for, we may need to get prints off it. And don't let ol' Teebo mess with it, either. That boy just loves to get his hands on any kind of vehicle, whether it runs or not.'

Ned chuckled. 'He's a borned mechanic, I got to say. But I'll warn him off. I don't think he's touched it yet — he's been guttin' a big ol' Caddy that come in last week with its side bashed in.'

Wash put down the phone and shrugged on his jacket again. It would probably be dark by the time he finished with this. Too late for the family outing, he was sure.

'Amy!' He stuck his head out into the hallway. 'Can you call my wife and tell her that I won't be home till late? Tell her I'll take her and the boy someplace tomorrow, if I can. I'm going on out to Ned's.'

★   ★   ★

The junk yard was a treasure of rusty refrigerators, remnants of old cars, wagon wheels, hoe-heads, and rakes without handles — not to mention every other sort of throwaway possible to imagine. Everything was sorted with painful neatness, each kind to itself, in rows or piles or whatever arrangement its anatomy dictated.

Shipp pulled up inside the chain-link-fenced enclosure, whose utilitarian skeleton was veiled by yellow jasmine vines a good part of the year. Already there were fragrant golden bells among the dark green foliage. He honked once and Ned waddled out, his round shape all but lost in overalls large enough to contain two of him.

'Over here, Sheriff,' he called, pointing to the part of the yard devoted to the corpses of cars and trucks.

Wash approached the dilapidated truck with hope and doubt. It would be too much luck to have that pickup turn up here, in his own front yard, so to speak. Yet Duson had been at the Frost house last night — he was sure of it. Who else would have been hiding in the myrtles, checking out the place? He could easily have driven the distance by yesterday afternoon. The plates were a match. Somehow he'd known they would be. The description was dead on.

'Good work, Ned,' he said, shaking the junk operator's grungy paw. 'I can understand you not making a fuss about papers on this clunker, but I sure am glad you heard that newscast. This is the very truck Duson stole.'

He had brought a plastic tarp, and with Ned's help he tied it over the truck to help preserve any prints or dust or other data that the specialists might pick up the next day. Then he rummaged in his wallet and pulled out a photocopy of a mug shot. 'Is this the man who sold it to you?'

The sun was down, and chilly darkness was creeping among the orderly rows of junk. 'Cain't see so good,' Ned said, squinting at the picture. 'Come on over here to the office, and I'll take a gander at it.'

The light in the office was all of forty watts, but it seemed enough. Ned took another glance and shook his head.

'It's kind of *like* him, but it's not the same man. The one that sold the truck was a lot older and skinnier, and the face was thinner, wrinkled up like a turtle, it was. He looked tired, somehow, not mean. This fella's younger and looks a hell of a lot meaner.'

Shipp looked at him in surprise. 'You dead certain of that? This is a picture of Duson that was taken the last time he was arrested. He might have lost weight since then.'

Ned held the photo closer to his face.

He turned it sideways, upside down, back right side up. He shook his head again

'No way this is the same man. Same *type*, yes. Head's shaped some the same. But the face is all wrong. The eyes are different. The chin is sharper. Just ain't the same man, Sheriff, and that's all I can say.'

'Then who in hell . . . ?' Shipp chopped off his words and sighed. 'Thanks, Ned. I'll sort this out some way, but damned if I know how, just yet. There'll be a man out in the morning to check for fingerprints and take samples. You'll be here?'

'Every day 'cept Sunday, Sheriff. You just tell him to blow three times, so I'll know it ain't Teebo, and I'll be out like a shot. You think you'll ketch that bastard?'

'I hope so. I certainly hope so. Thanks again, Ned. And good night.'

8

Martin had searched the big old Frost house thoroughly. Not once, but twice, he had gone through the whole place; every nook and cranny (and there had been more than he cared to think about) had been explored, without finding anything useful. Finally, weary and dusty, he retired back to the kitchen, where he heated up a cup of hot broth from a packet of dry mix he found in a cupboard. Deciding at last that it was safe to turn on a light, after pulling the old-fashioned green shades over the windows, he switched on the reading lamp sitting on the little desk in the corner.

He looked around. The big farm kitchen had obviously been completely remodeled, for comfort and convenience. It seemed to be a sort of all-purpose room, and evidently either Livingston Frost, or maybe even Lily herself, did the household bookkeeping at the desk.

After sipping at the broth, relishing its nourishing warmth, he got up and searched through the kitchen one more time, lackadaisically and without much hope. But this time he found a promising little twist of paper tucked way back in the corner of the desk drawer. He smoothed it out, and there, amongst a list which included a general practice doctor, an insurance agent, and the local grocery store, he found a circled phone number.

Beside it were two words which caught his attention: *Aunt Allison.* The area code was 318. He rummaged through the phone book looking for that number. There it was: the western half of Louisiana.

Without much hope, he called Information and asked in what city that particular number might be located. To his great surprise, he was not questioned about his motive, just given a swift reply. He tucked the note into his pocket.

After swishing out his broth cup and placing it carefully back in the cupboard, he glanced around to make certain he'd left no other tell-tale sign of his intrusion into the kitchen. Then he slid silently out the back door, relocking it carefully behind him.

He'd get to Bossier City somehow, hitch-hiking, if possible. Then he could walk on up to Plain Dealing, if he had to. A phone call to the aunt's place the next day might get him some directions. He could pretend to be some sort of repairman or maybe somebody calling about the fire insurance. Everybody got calls like that, and he had used that ploy plenty of times to gain entry into an unwitting victim's house.

He had recognized that name, 'Allison.' Lily Frost had but two relatives she spoke of with any fondness while they were together. One was her beloved brother Livingston — and the other was her grandfather's sister, whose name was Allison Vernier.

Martin Fewell was blessed with the kind of memory that allowed him never to forget anything that might be useful someday. And the information about the aunt had seemed important to him, in case Lily ever escaped from him. In the old days, he would have run her down and beaten anybody to a pulp who offered to interfere. Now his entire purpose had changed. He was a man on a mission — and, perhaps, he had discovered the key to that mission. Because where on earth would the Frosts have gone, except to kin? They had to be there, at the aunt's place. And he had to go there too.

He had decided that it was his job now, to make up for all his past sins. Keeping Lily safe was more important to him now than anything else. Since he'd heard about Duson's unsuccessful attack on Lily, his whole world had shrunk down to that single focus. He hoped to deal with Duson, in time, but first he had to safeguard Lily. Thinking about what he could do to her attacker would keep him warm all night.

In pitch darkness, he trudged away up the oil-top road, keeping himself oriented by the distant band of stars above the flanking treetops. His small bundle of newly acquired clothing seemed heavy

— and he was older than he used to be, but he didn't let either factor slow his steps. He'd get to Bossier City if he had to crawl on his hands and knees.

As it turned out, though, a freelance trucker with a load of heifers for a farmer in Tennessee picked him up on the highway before he'd walked more than a dozen miles. The fellow was sleepy, for he'd been driving all night, and he needed somebody to help him stay awake.

In the old days, Martin thought wryly, nobody in his right mind would have picked him up, because he used to be so big and tough and mean-looking. Now he only looked worn and weary, as he had noted in Lily's mirror. He was no threat to anyone. He was so thin and stooped that he didn't even seem big anymore — even to himself.

He talked randomly with the truck driver about all sorts of things as they bored through the night toward Shreveport. When they hit the interstate west of Shreveport, he ran out of talk — and besides, it was time to change off. It never paid to stick too long with one ride, even when you were setting out to do something honest for a change.

'If you can let me off close to the airport, that'd be real nice,' he said.

The driver nodded, wakeful now that daylight had come and there was enough traffic to keep him alert.

'Will do. Been nice to hear your stories. I never got to travel all that much. Just covered ground with the truck loaded and come back empty, like a yo-yo on a string. You okay for cash?'

Martin was startled. He'd forgotten, in all his years of muscle work and con games, that people sometimes cared to help each other. 'I'll be fine,' he said. 'Got an old aunt lives close to the airport, and that's where I'm headin'. Much obliged for the ride, though. Helped me out a lot.'

He stood by the side of the road, watching the rig pull away into the rising sun. Then he headed in to Bossier on foot, using the streets he remembered from his youth.

Actually, he had had an aunt, once, who lived somewhere near this place.

Things in the area had changed, of

course, even in the few years since he'd last come this way. But at least he knew where he was going and how to get there.

★   ★   ★

The sheriff had had a dream about that old pickup. He was out at the junkyard as soon as he'd checked the office and done the few major jobs waiting for him. Following him in a shiny van was Phil Taylor, on loan from the state. He had the forensic equipment with him to examine the truck from stem to stern.

'If there's a hair or a print or even a grain of dust there, I'll find it,' he promised as he approached the plastic-veiled vehicle. 'As it's crossed the state line, the Feds may be interested too. I'll keep you posted, Sheriff.'

Wash nodded as he backed out of the drive and headed back toward town. He had a feeling about that truck. If the driver wasn't Duson, who in hell could it be?

With the sudden impact of inspiration, he had an idea that propelled him toward his office with the sort of speed he often chided his deputies for using. Lily had thought Duson was Martin Fewell, back to harass her again, when he came into her kitchen. There had to be some kind of resemblance between them. Ned had said Duson's picture was similar to the man he'd seen, but definitely not the same person. Could, somehow, Martin Fewell have reentered the scene? How? And why? And for what possible reason would he have returned?

There was only one way to find out.

Shipp entered the building in an uncharacteristic rush and leaned over the desk where Amy was checking files. 'Amy, call Miz Vernier, will you? I need to talk to Lily immediately,' he said. 'I'll be in my office.'

When the call came through, he was staring at his filing cabinet as if to burn a hole in its gray-painted side. Something was bugging him, and he wasn't quite able to pin it down.

'Lily? Hi, there. Yes, things seem pretty quiet here, too. Listen, do you have a picture of Martin Fewell? I mean, here at the house where I might use the key you left to pick it up?'

'Why, no, Wash,' she said. 'I think I burned them all. But wouldn't you have one someplace in *your* files? He was wanted for quite a few years before they sent him up.'

She sounded worried, and he knew that old fear must be chipping away at her newfound sense of balance.

'Now why didn't I think of that? Of course — there ought to be something in the books. He was arrested here at least once, and if not, I can get a picture out of the morgue at the newspaper. Thanks, Lily-bird. You and Stony keep your wits about you, you hear?'

'Aunt Allison is carrying her pistol in her pocket. She may be ninety, but she'll take care of us if it kills her.' To his relief there was a hint of laughter in her voice.

He rummaged in the back files for the first year when Martin Fewell had run afoul of the law in Nichayac County. It actually wasn't all that far back, and Shipp soon had the thin sheaf of paperwork in hand. There was indeed a mug shot, but it didn't even come close to resembling the Martin Fewell that Shipp had known at the time.

It took him all morning to find a news photo that looked anything like the man. But he located one at last in the dusty files of the *Courier* and had Sue-Ann, the reporter-cum-girl Friday there, run him a photocopy that was passable. Then he headed back out to the junk yard.

When he handed Ned the punched-up photo copy, the junk dealer nodded. 'Yep, that's him. A bit younger and not so tired and skinny-lookin' — but that's the man.'

Something inside Wash resonated to the man's words. Somehow he had known that Fewell was going to come back into the picture, and here he was. But how did he fit? Was he acquainted with Myron Duson? Were they somehow related or in cahoots?

It might be that Lily Frost would know. Her lover might have talked about his convict friends, and Fewell and Duson had been in the same penitentiary for at least a short period of time that overlapped. His investigations into

181

Duson's career had told him that.

Wash returned to his office and dropped into his chair absentmindedly. He had no authority in Bossier Parish. The sheriff there was an unknown quantity. Going himself would seem officious, and his Louisiana counterpart would make that clear, he was certain. However, it might have been Fewell instead of Duson under that bush at the Frost house that night. And if so, he might have picked up some clue as to the whereabouts of the Frosts.

That same instinct told him that Allison Vernier's farm wasn't going to be as secure a hideout as they had all hoped. But he had no proof of anything, not even a real clue. How did you convince a skeptical official that you had a hunch there was going to be whole lot of trouble in his jurisdiction?

'With great difficulty,' he replied to himself. Then he dialed the Vernier number again, not wanting Amy to be a witness to his humiliation and uncertainty.

★ ★ ★

The newer roads up in this part of the country made Duson's trip much shorter than it would have been in the old days, when the highways seemed to go right through every pea-turkey little town and around their squares twice.

Duson had lifted a nice little Toyota in San Augustine, on the Texas side of the border. It was parked behind a gas station just waiting for its owner to show up after having it serviced and gassed. Now he whizzed along through the pine woods, noting the thin screens of standing timber that hid the devastation of loggers behind their scanty ranks.

He'd robbed a few loggers in his time, but they never had anything but grease and sweat on them. It had always puzzled Duson why anybody would work so hard for so little, when it was so easy to take what others sweated to earn. But he guessed it took all kinds, which made it nice for him. There wasn't all that much competition in his trade, and his stints in the slammer hadn't been all that bad. He'd made contacts, though the way this last job had turned out, he was about to decide that the quality of convicts was going down.

It wasn't easy to get good help, and that was a fact. Those idiots couldn't even hit a woman over the head hard enough to kill her anymore.

After a while he pulled over into a rest stop and studied his road map. Plain Dealing . . . it was a dinky little place, but not hard to find, and very close to Shreveport. As it was about time to change cars again, he waited, hiding behind a picnic table, until a couple pulled up in a newish Ford and headed, both at the same time, for the rest rooms. All you had to do was wait, he'd always known.

He sighed. At last things were going right again. He jiggered the lock with his special device and hot-wired the ignition in less time than he could have done the job with the keys. He slid out of the park and into traffic, already looking for the turnoff he wanted. Once he was headed for Plain Dealing and the northern part of the state, he became a little more cautious and took to the back roads again, blessing his long experience with dodging the law in these parts.

To his surprise, though, he passed two county cars on the way, both driven by men who seemed to be watching for somebody. He'd changed vehicles just in time, he realized. Probably was some local problem that had them stirred up like a nest of hornets.

*   *   *

Allison put down the receiver and sat staring out the window. Sheriff Shipp's disembodied voice echoed in her mind.

'Miz Allison,' he'd said, 'I hate to spring this on you like this, but we've got reason to believe Martin Fewell is headed out your way . . . '

'*Martin Fewell?*' A thrill of fear clutched her heart. 'What on earth would Martin Fewell be doin', headed out here?'

'That's just it, Miz Allison,' Wash said. 'I have no idea, but it would appear to me he's up to no good. Now, I've got no reason to think that . . . except . . . well, we both know what kind of relationship he had with Miss Lily. I hate to say it, but I wonder if he's not planning some sort of revenge on her . . . for leavin' him when she did.'

Allison was silent for a moment, pondering Wash's words. 'But how would he know she's here?'

'I just got through checking out the house. Seems like ol' Martin was in there and went through things pretty carefully. One thing I spotted was an advert referring to you and the farm. Looked like he'd laid it to one side. Now, in spite of his troubles, I never took Martin for an idiot. I s'pose he may have put two and two together and figured that might be where Miss Lily had gone.'

'What shall we do?'

'I'm on my way there now, but I have no idea what kind of a head start he may have on me. I've called Carl Weathers up at Shreveport. He said he'd try to get a couple of men over there as quick as he could.'

Allison had always considered Carl Weathers to be fairly worthless and lazy. But, she thought, any port in a storm . . .

'In the meantime,' Wash went on, 'I want the three of you to stay in and locked up. Stay together and arm yourselves with whatever you have available. Try to use your head, Miz Allison. I'm trustin' you to protect yourselves as best you can.'

'Thank you, Wash,' she said. 'I appreciate your concern. We'll make a stand, if need be. Won't be the first time I've had a challenge. Hopefully, it won't be the last.'

'I'll get there as soon as I can,' Wash said. 'Take care.' And then the line went silent.

Allison sat for a moment, gathering her thoughts. She picked up the phone and called down to the cabin at the end of the yard.

'Yes'm?' The old retainer's cracked voice betrayed she'd roused him from sleep.

'Sorry to wake you,' she said. 'We're going to have a quiet day here today. Just the three of us. I want you and the others to stay in and have a little rest yourselves. We won't need anything done up here at the house. We're just going to relax and take it easy. No point in having you all workin' either.'

'But what about your meals, Miz Allison? Won't you need something put together for . . . '

'Oh, no, that won't be necessary. I think there's cold cuts and potato salad in there. We'll just fix ourselves some sandwiches when we feel like it. I've been working everyone quite a bit. Time we all had ourselves a day of rest. You, too.'

'Well, all right, Miz Allison, if you say so. But if you need anythin' — anythin' at all, you just give us a shout, hear?'

'I surely will,' she said. 'But I doubt that'll be likely. Don't worry. We'll be fine.'

She felt a little better once she had taken care of the servants. No need in getting them involved in any of this.

'Stony! Lily!' she called down the hall toward their bedrooms. 'Time to get up now. I got news.'

*   *   *

Myron kept his foot pressed on the gas pedal, willing the stolen car to move as fast as possible across the terrain towards

Caddo Parish and Alexandria, Louisiana where Ms. Allison Frost Vernier lived.

He was certain now that there he would find the object of his quest: the tall, slender Frost woman who had confronted him during his most recent robbery attempt. She had had the gall to survive the Crowley twin's assault. It was mandatory that he silence her once and for all.

The engine hummed along all right, and he was relieved that this ride, at least, seemed to be holding up to the pace. Just a few more miles and he would be pulling into the town on the Red River. Then he would need to go to cover until dark. No need in being bold about it. Once there, he would have all the time in the world to case out the Vernier farm and zone in on his prey. After all, he mused, no one would ever guess he had run across that brief advertisement with the tell-tale name embedded in the fine print. The authorities would never suspect he could have tracked the Frosts down from such an unlikely clue.

Just for a moment, he wondered if he

was on a wild goose chase. What if this Vernier woman *wasn't* related to the Frosts? How could he be sure they had come all the way over here to Louisiana on the off chance he would come back to settle the score?

He shrugged. It didn't matter to him. He felt he was right with this hunch. If not, so what? He wouldn't have lost much . . . just some time. And maybe there would be valuable loot on the Vernier place in any case.

Duson was a firm believer in fate. And this felt like fate to him. Could be he would come out of this caper with a bigger payday than the original target. What was more, he reasoned, he was now on his own and wouldn't have to share the proceeds with any of those other losers.

Especially the Cajun. He grinned at the thought of the bloodied mess he'd left behind in the piny woods. That feller might lie there a good long time before any one ran across him. With no I.D., who knew when, or even if, he would ever be identified. And given

Frenchy's criminal record, they'd be hard put to tie Duson to the deed.

He relaxed back into the bucket seat. 'Pedal to the metal,' ran through his mind, and 'gas to the max.' Nothin' to do now but ride it out.

★   ★   ★

Carl Weathers had been somewhat skeptical about the desperate nature of his mission, but had finally agreed to meet him at the Vernier place ASAP.

'You say the old gal is in danger, Wash?' Carl asked again, and Wash could hear the doubt in the other man's voice.

'Carl, when have I ever steered you wrong?' He let the exasperation ring out. Washington Shipp was a man slow to anger, but when it warranted, he could stand toe to toe with the best of them.

'All right, all right. I'm convinced.' Carl turned away from the phone and barked out a few orders. 'Me and Duke will get right on down there. But I'm bettin' this is all just a joke of some sort. I just can't imagine someone goin' out after Miz

Allison. Everybody 'round these parts just loves that lady. If it's true, they'll have hell to pay comin' after the likes of her.'

'Just get down there as quick as you can, Carl,' Wash said. 'And Carl? Don't take nothin' for granted, hear? These bastards are serious bad guys. If harm is to be done, they're the ones to do it.'

With that, he slammed down the receiver, jammed his cap on his head and stormed out of the office. He met Whit Lambert at the car and stepped into the passenger side, preferring to leave the driving to the younger Lambert.

'Step on it, Whit,' he said as he strapped himself in. 'You put those rifles in the back?'

The young officer nodded. 'Yessir. And I made sure we've got plenty of ammo, too. This is really serious, isn't it?' There was a note of eagerness in his voice. Most days were pretty routine in their neck of the woods.

'Yep. It's serious all right. I just hope we, or Carl and his man, get there in time. We've got three helpless citizens out there countin' on us. It's about as serious as it's ever gonna get.'

Lambert buckled his own belt and revved up the motor. He'd also checked to make sure they had plenty of gas for the drive out to bayou country. There was a lot of space out there, and fill-up spots were few and far between.

'Siren?' Lambert's fingers hovered over the switch.

'Not yet. We've got a mite of road to cover. No need setting off alarms all along the way. Hold up on that thought. I'll let you know if I think we need to go in full tilt.'

'Sir.' Lambert's checked his mirrors and pulled carefully out into the street. Not much traffic this time of day, but no need in making a tough ride tougher.

As they pulled out on to the highway leading to the Louisiana border, Washington Shipp heaved a sigh of relief. Now he was in his element. On the trail of hardened criminals. Riding to the rescue of good people.

It don't get much better than this, he thought — and was immediately ashamed of it — but not too much.

9

Martin Fewell consulted the map again and began to drive slower, now that he was drawing closer to his goal.

The owner of the last little Mom-and-Pop service station he'd pulled into had been extremely helpful. 'Oh, Miz Vernier,' the man had crowed. 'Yes, she's a high-falutin' celebrity 'round these parts. Yessiree. The 'dog lady,' they call her. Has a real good reputation with all the animal folks in this part of the country — or so they tell me.'

'Is it much further to her place?' Martin asked, impatient to get the tank filled and on the road again.

'No, not what you'd call a far piece, by any means,' the man opined. And while Martin was counting out his change, the proprietor came up with a little map — the kind motels or cafés might hand out to tourists.

'Here.' He drew an imaginary line with

194

his grubby thumb. 'Just follow the main road for about ten more miles. There's a turn-off right there . . . ' He jabbed the paper at a small unnamed junction. 'Can't miss it. She's got her sign out there on the main highway. 'Course, you have to drive back in a ways off the road to get to the farm . . . it's a pretty drive back there in them piny woods . . . ' His voice trailed off as he pondered the possibilities of the scenery available at Miz Vernier's farm.

'Thanks, buddy,' Martin said, grabbing the tiny map out of the man's greasy paws. 'I owe you one.'

He had jumped back into the car and pulled out on to the highway, scattering gravel as he went. The service station man stood staring after him for a bit. *That 'ol guy was sure in one heck of a hurry*, he thought. *Wonder what that's all about?*

Martin knew he had broken the unwritten rule: never draw attention to yourself when you're planning a job. If law enforcement got wind of his mission out here, the geezer back at the station would be the first one in line to identify him. He knew that — and he didn't care. For the first time in his life he had something greater than his own agenda on his mind. He was old before his time, now, broken down by years of drug abuse, incarceration and living rough on the street.

But all that really mattered now was Lily. He suddenly realized that she had been the single most important and stabilizing factor in his whole rotten life — and he had thrown it all away. He had treated her about as bad as one person could treat another. And she had stayed with him, faithful and obedient right up until the end.

Right up until he had made that stupid mistake with Sam. He could still hear the pitiful sounds Sam had made during the fatal beating Martin had inflicted on him. And Lily had witnessed the whole thing. He did not want to think about all this, but he must. It was necessary to relive all the trauma, fear and anger he had felt in the months leading up to and during the trial. When Lily had turned on him like that, he had hated her for it. Now, he could understand that she had simply reached her cracking point.

So long as he was abusing her, beating her, making her the brunt of his own shortcomings, she stood by him. When he turned that abuse on another, it was more than she could bear. He got it now. He didn't blame her. Not one little bit. And if he could get to her, maybe act the hero for once in his godforsaken life, and save her from this fiend who was surely out to kill her. Maybe then, she would forgive him and he would reach some kind of peace with his inner demons.

But he had to get there first. He had to convince her she was in danger. And he had to act like a man for a change — not the drug-addled monster she remembered.

He began watching for the turnoff. The man said it was well-marked.

He only prayed he would be in time.

* * *

Myron Duson pulled to the side of the highway and peered down the winding side road leading, according to a small sign, to 'The Vernier Farm.' He had found the place!

He turned off the motor and sat there for a while, reflecting on the path that had led him here, and anticipating the final showdown to come.

He was sweating badly, a condition familiar to him from past such encounters. His heartbeat was steady but fast, his throat dry, and his eyes had a glazed-over look to them, as if he was viewing something far off in the distance.

He relished this moment, which he equated to that felt by some great hunter in the jungle stalking a wild beast. It was an exaltation of sorts, an excitement which thrust every nerve in his body into a tingle of something he could only describe as pure joy.

He went over all the events of the past few days again in his mind: the rush to put together the robbery crew; the failed attempt at the Frost house, including the stark fear in Lily Frost's eyes as she crumpled to the floor following the beating she received; and finally, the satisfying demise of Frenchy at his own hands. He shivered a bit in pleasure, recalling the solid *thunk* of the log against the Cajun's skull.

Suddenly his mind clicked into gear. What was it that the lanky woman had exclaimed when he first entered the kitchen the night of the robbery?

'Martin!' she had called out. 'Martin, don't hurt me!' Now why in the world would she call him 'Martin?'

He pondered that riddle a moment, then slapped his knee in glee. Now he knew why the man who had attacked him and stolen his truck alongside the road had struck a familiar chord. 'Martin' was Martin Fewell! And it all came rushing back to him in a flash.

Of course! His memory slipped back a few years, to a time when he had been incarcerated in one of the many prisons located near the border between Texas and Louisiana. He couldn't remember now exactly which state was involved in his arrest and trial, since he crossed the border so frequently, and had been arrested and served time so often. But it was a good-sized prison, and he was held there, cooling his heels for what seemed to him to be an eternity.

One day, during an exercise break in the yard, he was standing to one side, trying to get a breath of fresh air and mainly avoiding the other prisoners milling about like cattle in a slaughter-house. He had a tendency to look down on the others because, in his opinion, most of them were so stupid.

Suddenly he came face to face with an older man — and the two of them just stopped and stared at each other in dumb silence.

It is said, in some circles, that every human being on earth has a doppelgänger — a double; someone who resembles you so much you could be taken for twins. It is not often you run into such a person unexpectedly, but that is exactly what had happened to Myron Duson and Martin Fewell on that fateful day.

'Well, I'll be damned . . . ' were the first words out of Myron's mouth. 'Who the *hell* are you — and where in the hell did you come from?'

Martin wasn't an exact match to Myron. For one thing, there was a distinct difference in their ages. Martin, who had been tall and imposing in his younger days, had shrunk several inches and was now bent over with a severe and somewhat debilitating hump on his back. There were threads of gray running through his once-inky hair, and his face was creased with wear and tear, the result of years of drug abuse and living rough on the street.

Myron, on the other hand, was still virile and erect to his full height, a mountain of a man. His face remained wrinkle-free, except for a few crinkles around his eyes, and his hair was full and black as a raven's wing.

Other than that, they could have been brothers. Shaking his head, Martin, shrugged then gestured toward one of the empty picnic benches in a shaded corner of the yard.

'Care to have a chat?' he said.

'Sure, don't mind if I do,' Duson replied. Once seated, he offered up a cigarette from the half-used pack in his shirt pocket. 'Smoke?'

Martin accepted, and the two bent over the shared match Myron proffered.

'Name? Or would you prefer that be off limits?' He inhaled deeply and sent a smoke ring or two drifting off into the aether.

'Naw, I'm okay with that. I'm Martin Fewell. I ain't got nothin' to hide . . . or not much at least,' he said with a grin at his own attempt at humor.

'I'm Myron Duson. Pleased to make your acquaintance.' He pronounced it 'Dew-sew' in the Cajun manner, with the emphasis on the final syllable. Although most of the time he answered to 'Dew-zun' as he was usually called these days. 'I guess we got ourselves what you might call a quandary,' he added.

'You might say that,' Fewell acknowledged, sending his own smoke signals to the sky. 'Where do you hail from, if you don't mind my askin'?'

'Oh, here and there.' Duson didn't want to give away too much just yet. 'Mostly over in bayou country. But I get around. I don't have any particular place I call home.'

'Same here. Although I stick mainly to east Texas. Have been known to cross the border from time to time, but mostly I hang around these parts. The evil you know . . . ' Martin laughed again at his little joke.

Duson smiled. The guy was beginning to get on his nerves, but he was still curious about him. He was always interested in any bit of information he might turn to profit at some point in time. This seemed like one of those possibilities. He didn't know yet how he might be able to use this geezer, but if there was a way, Myron Duson was the man to find it.

Now, years later, sitting here by the side of the road, Myron continued to think back about that conversation with his 'twin' back in prison. They had exchanged a bit of background information, as Martin, more than Myron, seemed almost eager to find a willing listener to his story. He shared a general dissatisfaction with his lot in life, placing blame squarely on the backs of others, primarily all his family members, the schools, the judicial system — and especially one Miss Lily Frost — who, he assured Dyson, had completely ruined his life.

'If it hadn't been for her, and her high-falutin' kinfolk . . . ' he said, picking a bit of tobacco from what was left of his front teeth, ' . . . if it hadn't been for her, I wouldn't be sittin' here now. She led me down the road to perdition, I swear. I wouldn't have done half the things I did if I hadn't been tryin' to make a pile a money to support her and her habit.' He glanced sideways at Myron to see how the other man responded to this bunch of malarkey.

'Well, now,' said Myron, leaning back a bit on the bench and stretching his arms out to relieve a kink. 'I can't say as I've had the same experience. Most of my lady friends have been just that . . . friends with benefits.' He winked at Martin, who snickered and nodded.

'Yessir,' the older man replied. 'And that's the way they ought to be treated, too. Once you start spoilin' them, they never let you forget it. Yup, I made a real mistake with that one. If I ever get a chance, I'm going back and look her up. I'll teach her about 'benefits' all right.'

They'd both had a laugh over that. But now Myron thought about it some more. What if Martin Fewell *had* come back to look up Lily? What if he had threatened her, by phone or by mail? Would there be a record of that somewhere?

As always, he worried and fretted the bit of information, trying to tease an advantage out of it. What if . . . ? What if Martin Fewell was on his way, or even now was at the Vernier Farm? What if he had made the same connection as Myron, and was headed there to take his revenge on Lily, just like Myron hoped to do? What possible advantage could that knowledge be to him?

And then it came to him. So simple and easy he laughed out loud at the beauty of it. If Martin Fewell, the old geezer he'd met by chance who resembled him so much, and who had an actual known relationship with Lily

Frost — if he had figured out where she'd gone to ground, wouldn't this be the key to Myron Duson's plan? He was going to do this deed no matter what, but if Martin beat him to it, or showed up during or after the process, how easy would it be to add him to the list? The authorities would find Lily, her crippled brother, her ancient aunt — and her estranged lover. All in one bloody heap.

There could be no other conclusion than Martin Fewell had come to the farm in a fit of rage and had killed all three people. Then, regretting his act of violence, he had taken his own life. The authorities would be satisfied with that story, Myron felt sure. And he would have gotten away with the perfect murder — and no witnesses would survive to tell the tale.

Humming a little tune, he pulled his pistol out of his jacket and laid it on the seat next to him. He started the motor, smiling a bit at the satisfying purr of the engine. Looking both ways — no point in a stupid accident at this juncture

— Myron Duson turned off the road and headed towards his fate.

* * *

Lily stood frozen, staring out the front window of the farmhouse belonging to her great-aunt. Her face was pinched and pale. The fingers holding back the curtain were clenched tightly, and her tall, slender body was erect and taut.

When Allison had raised the alarm earlier, she had emerged from a restless dream-filled sleep which had given her no peace. Pursued by faceless monsters, she had run from pillar to post, seeking refuge in the most unlikely places. As she woke, her last thought had been, 'Where is Stony? I must find Stony.'

Stony, of course, was behind her in the room, seated with Allison at the round oak table, sipping at his second or third cup of steaming black coffee. Ordinarily, he refrained from overdoing the caffeine, maintaining it made his angina worse. But today, he felt the need for an additional burst of energy.

'See anything out there?' Allison called out. Her voice, though thin, did not waver, and there was the strength of resolve in its timbre.

'Nope. Not a thing. I haven't even seen a bird rise.' Lily turned away from the window and flounced restlessly on a small divan covered in a flowery print shoved in front of the window to take advantage of the morning light.

'Now, are we all clear on a strategy?' Stony put his cup down with a clink. 'Do we all know what we're going to do?'

Lily rolled her eyes. They had been over their plans for survival so many times she was afraid she would become too complaisant and ruin it all by not staying alert to any strange noise or occurrence. 'I'm to stand in front of you two and lure the . . . (she had trouble with this image) . . . lure the attacker in by asking him questions and appealing to his conscience.' She grimaced. 'As if he has any such thing as a conscience!'

'Yes,' her brother agreed. 'Although I want you to try and keep out of his reach, if at all possible. The last thing we want is for him to grab you and try to hold you as some sort of hostage.'

'Agreed,' Lily said. 'I definitely do *not* want to become a hostage!'

'Then, when his attention is on you, or you have him involved in some sort of conversation, Aunt Allison will stumble to one side. When he looks at her, I'll pull out my rifle-cane and shoot, hopefully striking him in a vital area. Allison, in the meantime, will have her pistol ready in her pocket and will fire at him at the same time, aiming for his head or heart, whichever spot seems most likely to her. You, of course, will duck out of the way.'

'Got it,' Lily replied. 'Oh, my, how I wish this was all over with and we were sitting here having our supper tonight, all safe and sound!'

'Just hold that thought, the both of you.' Allison, her primed pistol burning a hole in her pocket as she spoke, looked anxiously from one to the other.

'Oh, yes, my dears. Please hold on to that thought. This will all be over in a few hours, I think. With any luck, either Carl

Weathers or Wash Shipp will be here soon. They'll take care of us then.'

The words to an old tune, 'Someone to Watch over Me,' echoed in Lily's ears. She didn't know if it was actually playing on the little portable radio perched on the end table near the sofa — or if she was having another one of those pesky flashbacks, where her mind wandered uncontrollably through past episodes of her earlier life.

It didn't matter. None of it mattered really, she thought. Except for Stony and Aunt Allison. Why oh why did those two innocent souls have to be dragged into this mess? And it was all her fault. If only she hadn't gotten tangled up with that idiot, Martin Fewell.

But, she reminded herself, it was *not* her fault about the other one . . . the unknown assailant who looked so much like Martin. Those men, she knew now, were after Stony's guns. And she had nothing to do with that. She could not be blamed if that monster had come looking for her to make sure she could never identify him.

She sat up a little straighter. It was her turn to be the hero. She could either hold up her end of the deal and give Stony and Allison a chance to put an end to this nightmare . . . or she could crumble into a dismal failure once again, putting the burden back on those who didn't deserve it.

It really was her choice now. She glanced over at the end table again. Yes, there was the radio, already tuned to the music station Aunt Allison enjoyed during her afternoon siesta here in the warm, comfortable room with the sunlight streaming in.

There also were the writing tools, pen, stationery in a little folder, and a tiny round brass stamp dispenser. In off moments, her aunt would sit here and compose the letters she sent out to friends, other breeders, potential customers. Her charming, chatty notes had endeared her to every one of her regular correspondents, and were a good part of her successful business strategy.

The final item that caught Lily's eye also caught a ray of sun, almost blinding her, as she stared at it, fixated. With a quick catlike movement, totally unlike her usual slow and measured pace, she rose, turned to the table, her back to the others, and grabbed the shiny object. Stuffing it into her slacks pocket, she took a seat at the table and poured herself a cup of coffee.

'All right,' she said, adding a heaping spoonful of sugar, 'I think we're all ready for whatever's to come.'

Just then, a commotion arose out near the kennels and several of the dogs began to bark and howl nervously. Aunt Allison half rose out of her chair, concern etching her face. 'Someone's out there,' she said. 'I guess it's begun.'

All three rose as one and made their way out into the darkened hallway. Lily blinked her eyes rapidly to focus. Without a word to the others, she went straight to the carved oaken door, turned the double bolt, and opened the polished knob. She stepped out on to the honed wooden planks of the veranda, paused to get her bearings, then went straight to the wide front steps which traced majestic curves down to the graveled drive beyond.

She assumed the other two were behind her, flanking her on either side, weapons at the ready. What they didn't know was that she, too, had a weapon of her own . . . and every intention of using it.

A figure loomed up in front of her as she reached the bottom step, and she caught her breath. He wasn't as tall as she remembered, and he seemed — somehow — less menacing, and more vulnerable.

'Well, Lily,' he drawled, 'long time, no see. How ya been keepin' yourself?'

'What are you doing here, Martin?' she said evenly, watching his every move carefully.

'I got a score to settle with you, Lily. I think you know that . . . ' He made a slight move toward her and she gasped.

Without thinking, she grabbed the object from her pocket, raised it high above her head and brought it down in a slashing motion. She had aimed for the left side of his chest. She felt a *clunk* of resistance, as if she had hit something solid. She pulled back a bit, lowered her aim, and struck again.

This time her weapon found its mark, sliding between the ribs . . . just as if she were boning a roast for the dinner table.

'*Ugh!*' Martin looked at her quizzically for a moment. 'Lily,' he whispered, so low she could scarcely hear him. 'Oh, my. You've changed, haven't you?'

Before he slumped to the ground, he added, 'But I didn't mean you no harm . . . really . . . I . . . '

Whatever his last thought was, it was shared between him and his Maker.

Lily looked down at the rumpled pile of clothing at her feet. She had no feeling at this moment. She was numb with the magnitude of it all.

'Lily!' Stony grabbed her and pulled her away. 'What on earth . . . ?'

Allison stared down at what was left of Martin Fewell and the shiny object protruding from his chest. An intricate chased handle graced the part she could see.

'Father's letter-opener,' she said. 'Oh, Lily.'

The three stood there silently.

Finally, Stony raised his head. 'One down,' he said. 'Where's the other one?'

'Right here,' came a deep voice, and a giant figure stepped out from behind the overgrown lilac bush at the corner of the porch. 'I'm the other one . . . and here I am. You've done part of my job for me.'

'Who are you?' Stony demanded of the newcomer. He motioned slightly to Lily and Allison, and the two attempted to reassemble according to their original plan. It was a little difficult to pull off, what with Martin lying there stone-cold dead in front of them. But they all three wheeled around to face the new threat, Lily slightly in front of Allison and Stony. With any luck, they could still pull it off.

'Me? I'm your worst nightmare,' Myron Duson said. He stood head and shoulders above all three of them, and with Martin safely dispatched, he knew he was in complete control of the situation.

Lily cleared her throat. It was her turn. 'You're one of the men who robbed us and beat me, back at our house in Texas,' she said. 'You got what you wanted then. What more do you want with us?' She

215

thought she knew, but she had to keep him talking.

'Well, that's just it. Those guns weren't what we were lookin' for. They were all just for show. The real stuff must be hidden away somewhere else.' He looked over at Stony, standing just behind Lily on the right. 'I can make you a deal, I guess,' Duson went on, speaking directly to the cripple now. 'I can guarantee these ladies safe passage . . . I won't touch a hair of their heads. But you've got to take me where those expensive guns are. The ladies or your guns. That's gonna be your choice, gimp.'

At the last word, something in Stony snapped. He knew, without a doubt in the world, that Duson was lying to him. He had no intention of letting any of them go. He was just looking for something to sweeten the pot — the location of Stony's expensive collection.

'By Christ, you'll not get anything from us!' Stony shouted. At the same moment he made a lunge forward, drawing his rifle cane up and out of its sheath. With one mighty thrust, knowing he would be hard put to reach the giant's chest or other vital organs, he aimed the gun directly at Myron Duson's thigh, hoping to hit the femoral artery, and pulled the firing mechanism.

'*Aiee!*' Duson screamed, falling backwards from the force of Stony's shot. He reached toward his belt, but Stony beat him to it, parrying the bigger man's hand away from the stashed pistol with the tip of the rifle.

Duson writhed on the ground, blood spurting from the slashed artery. 'Help me,' he pleaded.

Stony looked at Lily and she nodded. He reached down, unbuckled his belt and pulled it off his skinny frame. He handed the rifle to Lily, kicked the pistol out of the way then knelt down to apply the strap around the man's upper leg as a tourniquet.

'There,' he said finally. 'That should hold for a bit. At least until the law arrives and decides what to do about this piece of shit.'

Allison had been standing to one side. Now she lifted her head. 'I smell smoke!'

she said. 'Something's on fire!'

'I did it,' croaked Duson, a half-smile flickering on his ashen lips. 'I set your damned kennel on fire. Those fancy dogs of yours don't stand a chance.'

'No!' Allison turned and flew down the path toward the kennels. Her precious dogs! She couldn't bear the thought of the agony they would endure being burned alive.

'You filthy bastard!' Stony stared helplessly after his aunt. Sure enough, a slight wisp of smoke could be seen lazily drifting into the sky above the kennels. 'I oughta take this belt off you — let you die like the dog you are!'

Just then, the sound of sirens echoed through the piny woods. Carl Weathers, followed closely by Wash Shipp, were making tracks toward the Vernier farm.

Help was on the way.

10

No one was more surprised than Wash Shipp when Whit Lambert rounded the bend and entered the driveway leading up to Allison Vernier's house. Both he and Carl Weathers had switched on their sirens when they had run across the two cars abandoned by Martin Fewell and Myron Duson on the way into the yard. But neither was prepared for the scene that awaited them.

Lily stood like an Amazon goddess, rifle-cane in hand, guarding the stricken Myron Duson. Stony Frost was pacing nearby, debating whether to go after his aunt and help her at the kennels or stand his ground in case Duson revived enough to attempt an escape. Off to one side was a crumpled mess which was revealed to be the dead body of Martin Fewell. Blood was spattered everywhere, including on Lily and Stony, who appeared oblivious to it.

'Where's Miz Allison?' Carl cried to them. 'Is she all right?'

'The kennels.' Stony managed to point a shaking figure in the direction of the outbuildings. 'This idiot set them on fire. She's trying to save the dogs . . . '

Without a further word, Carl and his assistant ran off in the direction of the kennels. Stony could only pray they wouldn't be too late.

'What happened, Lily?' Wash said anxiously, bending down to examine Duson's wound. He took the precaution of handcuffing the giant's wrists in front of him. Nodding, he checked the makeshift tourniquet and turned to Lambert. 'Get those EMTs out here, STAT,' he shouted. 'This man's critical.'

Whit Lambert rumbled into the radio speaker, contacting the ambulance and EMT crew following at a slower pace behind. 'Hurry it up, guys,' he said. 'We've got a man down here.'

'Go on, Stony,' Wash said. 'Go see about Miz Allison. We can handle this here.'

Without a word, Stony turned toward

the kennels and painfully hobbled in that direction. A faint wisp of smoke was making its way up through the pine trees. Thankfully, he noted, it appeared to be dissipating rapidly, and there was no sign of the heavy black smoke that would indicate a major fire was underway.

'Now, Miz Lily . . . ' Wash turned to the grim-faced woman still standing guard and gently removed Stony's rifle-cane from her grasp. ' . . . what on earth happened here?' He motioned at the lifeless body of Martin Fewell. 'Did he threaten y'all?'

Lily turned a tear-stained face to the officer. 'Sheriff . . . there's something I need to say about this. I'm trying to get it straight in my own mind . . . and I will . . . but something's not right here. And I need to explain it . . . '

'Hush, now,' Wash rumbled. 'Sit down here on the stoop and let's think about this a minute. I suspect this all happened very quickly . . . am I right?' She nodded, taking a seat on the top step. 'And I also suspect you didn't have a real clear idea of who either one of these men was

. . . not right away at least.'

She looked at him, but didn't answer.

'All right, then. Let's just take our time about all this. We'll get this all sorted out in due course. But Miz Lily . . . I don't want you to go blamin' yourself for any of this, hear? None of this was your fault — none of it.' He stopped then, patted her shoulder, and continued to keep an eye on the ashen Duson until Lambert came back from directing the ambulance in to the dooryard. He watched as the EMTs checked Duson's vitals, began an IV line and carefully lifted him to the gurney and on into the ambulance.

Carl Weathers returned from the kennels and gave the ambulance crew instructions about dealing with Duson at the town medical center. His assistant would ride with them to provide security.

'Well,' he said, turning to Wash. 'The good news is that fire didn't go nowhere. It was damp at the corner of the building where he tried to start it, so it burned a bit, but never took hold. Miz Allison is looking after her dogs, with Mr. Frost's help. They all seem to have survived just fine.'

'That's good news, Carl.' Wash gestured over at Martin's body. 'There's the not-so-good news. That's one Martin Fewell. He was the sonofagun who tried to ruin Miz Lily's life. God knows why he showed up now — but I do believe the lady felt she had to defend herself.' He looked Carl Weathers straight in the eye. 'Looks to me like a pretty straightforward case of self-defense. Wouldn't you say?'

Carl Weathers looked at the body lying stone-cold on the ground, then at the pale face of Lily Frost, hugging her knees and rocking back and forth on the top step of the porch.

'You called it, Wash. I ain't one to argue about such things. I think we can write this one up as self-defense, pure and simple.'

★   ★   ★

Allison Vernier's private physician was called and rushed out to the house as quickly as he could. While he was

223

checking out the old lady and going over her vital signs, the household staff was summoned and began picking up the pieces to get everything humming again.

Soon, an urn of hot black coffee stood ready on the sideboard, and a meal of cold sandwiches and a vat of steaming soup was quickly prepared for the emergency teams and anyone else who needed nourishment and a moment to rest.

Lily and Stony sat to one side, quietly surveying the activity spinning around them. Both seemed to be in a state of shock, a natural result of all the stress leading up to the final confrontation. Wash couldn't help but notice how distant and sad Lily seemed. He had a hunch about that, but would pick the best time to talk to her privately.

Once the coroner had arrived, checked Martin Fewell's body for the final time, and ordered it carried off in the county hearse, Washington Shipp heaved a sigh of relief. Myron Duson, ashen with loss of blood, was bundled up by the EMTs and strapped into the back of the ambulance.

Carl Weathers's deputy rode with Duson, with stern and detailed instructions to monitor their prisoner at all times, even as he was undergoing the necessary emergency surgery.

With any luck, Wash thought, the parish inquests, both here and in Bossier, would go smoothly. Both sheriffs would be cooperative, he felt sure. But he would have to have a long honest talk with Lily and Stony, and get them on board for just how things had gone down — but he thought he could talk sense to them.

He had a pretty good idea of how it had all played out. Allison, Stony and Lily had put together a pretty good plan for defending themselves. And Lily, for whatever reason, had been the strongest one of them all — something that somewhat surprised him.

Poor old Martin Fewell, Wash thought. Coming here seeking — what? Redemption, maybe? Had just been in the wrong spot at the wrong time.

But Washington Shipp did not waste any time or effort worrying about whether or not Lily had killed Fewell outright

— or had, indeed, been afraid for her life. He also considered how fearful she may have been for the safety of her brother and their aunt.

No. He had the whole scenario pretty straight in his head. This family had suffered enough . . . especially Lily. He saw no justice in putting them through a prolonged murder trial unnecessarily. They would endure enough trauma in their lives from this incident as it was.

But, he thought, from what he was seeing here, they would get through it all and come out on the other side intact. Old Miz Allison seemed willing, almost eager, to welcome Stony and Lily into her household for as long as they wanted to be there.

And the brother and sister, if anything, seemed much stronger, more resilient, and more confident than he ever would have believed possible. This affair, as horrible as it was, could well mark a new beginning for this family — one that would keep them together, safe and strong, and content even, for years to come. And that was a good thing.

They're like a Frost line, he thought. *Their roots run very deep, and that line of frost is thick and solid enough to protect them from this and all other challenges.*

Washington Shipp looked around at the bustling scene and stood.

Time to head home to his own family. His job here was done.

THE RED TAPE MURDERS

Gerald Verner

Superintendent Budd's latest murder investigation begins with the murder of a solicitor, found strangled with red tape. Soon, two more local solicitors are murdered in similar fashion. Eventually Budd learns that two years earlier, a man shot himself when about to lose the bungalow he built, under a compulsory purchase order of the council. Two of the solicitors had acted in the sale of the land, and the third had acted for the council. Is someone seeking vengeance for the man who committed suicide — himself a victim of red tape?

REDEMPTION TRAIL

Victor Rosseau

Petty criminal Alfred Collins finds himself the victim of a conspiracy to frame him for murder. Sentenced to twenty years in prison, he manages to effect a daring escape, and assumes a new identity. Eventually he learns that the man who framed him has fled to work for a lumbering company. Consumed with the passion for revenge and the thought of being able to force a confession that would clear his name and free him from the life of a fugitive, Collins follows his trail into the Canadian wilderness . . .

LORD JAMES HARRINGTON AND THE AUTUMN MYSTERY

Lynn Florkiewicz

James and his wife Beth are helping with harvest festivities when they learn that escaped convict Locksmith Joe, a known killer, is in the area. Also, new arrivals Christie Cameron and his sister Jeannie refuse to integrate into the community and have upset a number of villagers. When Christie is found dead in his bedroom, clues suggest foul play, yet the room was locked from the inside. How did the killer get in? Was Locksmith Joe involved? Then a second death occurs, and James puts his sleuthing hat on . . .

THE PIEMAN'S LAST SONG

Tony Gleeson

The Tennessee Pieman was a beloved celebrity until he disappeared into seclusion near a small town. Now he's turned up murdered, his body discovered inside a garage on his ranch, and local police chief Wilma Acosta has assembled a bizarre list of likely suspects: employees who all seem to be harboring their own mysterious secrets. Despite her doubts about whether she's up to the task, if anybody can find the hidden killer among the perplexing cast of characters on hand, it will have to be the intrepid Wilma.